# THE QUIET TIME

# THE QUIET TIME

*To Tom!*
*Fellow lover of*
*words who knows of*
*the importance of*
*quiet time.*
*Warmly,*

*12/9/14*

## STORIES BY DIMITRI KERIOTIS

STEPHEN F. AUSTIN STATE UNIVERSITY PRESS
NACOGDOCHES, TEXAS

Versions of some stories in this collection have appeared in the following journals:
"Barking Dog": *Beloit Fiction Journal;* "Kevin Sinclair": *BorderSenses;* "Bride Finder":
*Minnetonka Review;* "Red Rock Canyon" (previously titled "Betrayed"): *Penumbra;*
"Waiting": *Evening Street Review,* "The Short Reign of Chef Gerard": *Epicenter,*
"Fleeing": *Flyway;* "The Quiet Time": *Georgetown Review.*

Stephen F. Austin State University Press
1936 North Street, LAN 203
Nacogdoches, TX 75962

sfapress@sfasu.edu

Book Design: Troy Varvel
Cover Art: Anastasia Keriotis
Cover Design: Troy Varvel

LIBRARY OF CONGRESS CATALOGUING-IN-PUBLICATION DATA

Keriotis, Dimitri
The Quiet Time: Stories/Dimitri Keriotis—1st ed.
p.cm.
ISBN: 978-1-62288-073-7

I. Title

First Edition: 2014

# TABLE OF CONTENTS

Barking Dog   9

Kevin Sinclair   19

Bride Finder   25

The Wedding Apartment   45

Weighing the Options   65

Red Rock Canyon   80

The Quiet Time   89

Waiting   96

The Short Reign of Chef Gerard   107

Thrown out in Thessaloniki   121

Fleeing   140

*For my mother*

# Acknowledgements

Thanks to the team at SFA Press, especially Troy Varvel, for the care in leading this book and its author through the publication journey.

Many thanks to the following individuals who helped shape one or more of these stories: Mike Smedshammer, Gabi Steiner, Michael Strangio, Paul Neumann, Jeanne Herasemovitch, Rick Rivera, Mike Branch, Dipali Murti, Fred Arroyo, and the boys at Querencia: BB, JP, and KC.

Thanks to my Sub Club brothers, Sam Pierstorff and Optimism One, whose camaraderie took submitting the manuscript to the next level. Additional thanks to Sam, whose advice over the years has made the difference.

My continual thanks to my family members, immediate and extended, for all their encouragement.

Heartfelt thanks to 'Ike, whose incessant support and affirmations continue to move me and my work in the right direction.

Enormous gratitude to my writing teachers: Paul Eggers, Steve Gutierrez, Doug Rice, and the late Raymond Federer. Special thanks goes to Daniel Chacon for his helpful feedback and counsel, and to Ben Percy, a man of his word, who stood by this project and provided pivotal attention along the way. To my main teacher, Rob Davidson, whose guidance knows no bounds, infinite thanks aren't enough.

To the late Brenda "BC" Robert, who read and critiqued most of these stories multiple times, this book is teeming with your editorial touches. Yours is a loss greatly felt.

Finally, my greatest thanks goes to my first and final reader, my wife Ingrid, whose knowing eye and undying support have been essential in sustaining my writing life. This writer and man would be lost without you.

# BARKING DOG

Evelyn looked up from washing potatoes to see their neighbor coming up the long walkway. What's he want? she thought. He wore brown cords and a loud shirt from Africa or India or God knows where. The Doberman tethered near their barn lunged and barked. She and Herb had met the neighbor and his wife two years ago, before they had a baby. They'd introduced themselves while returning from a walk along the two-lane county road, said they'd moved out to the country to be in nature, said he taught at the local university. After that Evelyn often spotted them from her house—a clean diagonal shot across a long stretch of lawn and the road. A world flag hung from their porch. They drove Toyota hybrids.

Evelyn slid out of the kitchen, drying her hands on her apron. She stood next to the mirror in the dark entryway, shifting her weight away from her bad hip. The neighbor's silhouette appeared in the door's yellow privacy glass. She knew he couldn't see her. The Doberman barked. The doorbell rang. She kept still and breathed out of her nose. The Doberman barked. Herb had always kept a guard dog alongside the white barn that housed his shop and equipment. He hired Mexicans seasonally to work the 300-acre peach orchard that wrapped around three sides of their house. In the spring after Herb disked the soil, every two weeks the Mexicans moved metal irrigation pipe two rows over so that Herb could flood irrigate parts of his orchard. In the summer the Mexicans climbed their aluminum ladders to pick the peaches, dropping them into sacks that hung from their shoulders, and then dumping their loads into wooden bins sitting in the orchard rows. In the winter they pruned the trees with pole saws, slicing suckers from around trunks, cutting off knobby infected branches and rock-hard dead limbs. Herb had told Evelyn that if the dog weren't out near the barn, those people would take his tools, tractor, spray rig, everything. After she had miscarried in their third year of marriage, she asked if she could get a little dog, a pet to keep her company in the house while he was out working. He shook his head. "One dog's enough."

The doorbell rang again. Evelyn stood very still. The neighbor rang the bell two more times and then walked away. The Doberman growled and barked. "Good," Evelyn said.

She turned and saw the face of an old woman in the mirror: her eyelids drooped, deep lines cut into the sides of her chin, the skin on her neck sagged. She dyed her hair brown to cover up the gray, but it didn't make a difference. Evelyn knew she looked like an old woman. Other women didn't look so old at 63, why did she? At least she'd stayed thin. She still fit into the same sized cotton blouses and jeans she wore when Herb brought her out to the country 44 years before—a small victory.

Why would he come to their door? She'd seen him mowing his lawn and sitting on the front porch with his wife. She'd seen them flood irrigate their one-acre pasture, the woman out in her rubber boots turning the valves. At the end of their first summer in the country, the petite woman was pregnant.

Evelyn had always wanted to feel a child grow inside of her. She'd wanted to have at least one child, but Herb said, "We have enough work out here without any kids." Evelyn hadn't responded, but she stopped putting in her diaphragm and didn't tell Herb. She'd give him an extra beer in the evening and sit close to him as he watched a Western or cop show, and later he'd climb on top of her. Two months later she missed her period. She threw up every time diesel exhaust from Herb's tractor crept into the house. She worried that he would suspect something. One morning he asked her, "You sure seem sick. Why don't you go to the doctor?"

"I will if it doesn't pass soon," she said.

He nodded and went out to the barn to wrench on a tractor. While window shopping downtown she spotted a wooden crib. She put it on lay-away but felt guilty because Herb still didn't know. She decided next month she'd tell him. Seven weeks into her pregnancy, she awoke with a cramp in her abdomen. Herb's leafless peach trees stood in a sea of fog. Pounding drummed the air. Herb was in the barn breaking apart bad wooden bins. She'd seen him do it every winter. Forged steel hitting wood. He'd first smash the 4x4 corners and cross supports with his sledge hammer and then would attack the walls, sometimes penetrating them, leaving big holes, and he'd keep at it until all that was left of the bin was a splintered pile of wood. Then he'd hammer away on another. The pain grew more intense in Evelyn. She said, "Oh, God," and rubbed her lower abdomen as she ran to the bathroom. Herb's sledge pounded and pounded like a piston. Evelyn doubled over in front of the sink. "Please, no." Herb smashed the bin over and over, and then the pounding stopped. Evelyn held herself and rubbed. Then she felt it break loose, like the side of a hill a home sits on. She felt the blood before struggling to the toilet and sitting down. She doubled over and wept as her body discharged thick, bloody tissue. She bent down to look, blinking to see. She kneeled and fished it from the toilet and cupped it in her hands. Rocking on her knees, she wept and stared at it. When she couldn't cry anymore and it felt like acid had pooled in her stomach, she spread her fingers and let her hope fall into the toilet. She flushed it, watching it turn round and round until it was gone.

When Herb came in an hour later, she was in bed staring at the wall.

"Hon, are you okay?" he said, coming around to her side of the bed.

"I'll be all right."

He felt her forehead. "You feel a little warm. How about a glass of water?"

"Okay."

She never told anyone. And she never tried again.

Evelyn had watched the neighbor's pregnant wife water plants, clip grape vines, sweep the porch. The woman seemed comfortable with herself, even wearing a camisole without a bra. Evelyn liked that feeling of freedom when she put on her nightgown, but being outside or around the house like that was something different. She placed the potatoes on a rack, dried her hands, and pulled a T-bone steak from the fridge and frozen peas from the freezer. She'd wanted to take the neighbors a plate of cookies when they moved in but changed her mind when they stuck an Obama sign on their lawn.

Herb came through the back door and hung his baseball cap on a dining room chair next to the windows. His wrinkled face was dusty, as were his old button-down shirt and jeans. His bald head peeked out of his gray comb-over.

"How many times have I told you that I don't want your dusty things in the house?"

"Give me some water," he said, taking off his boots.

"I mopped today. Put those outside." She filled a glass from the faucet and set it on the counter.

He dropped his boots and cap on the back stoop and grabbed the glass of water.

"That liberal neighbor was just here. He didn't see me, and I didn't open the door."

Herb handed her the empty glass. "Huh," he said and walked down the carpeted hall.

The previous spring the neighbors had replaced their front lawn with a garden. Herb said, "They're smart. It's better to grow food than grass. We should make our garden bigger by ripping out our lawn." Evelyn saw that the woman had planted tomatoes. She wanted to tell her that Beefsteaks did best in their soil, but Herb believed that people needed to figure things out on their own, so she didn't.

The neighbor's wife had the baby soon after they'd planted their garden. Mornings and evenings Evelyn watched her push the stroller up the county road and turn onto the main dirt road of Herb's orchard. She looked calm, serene, like she liked her life. Herb complained to Evelyn, saying, "If she trips on our property, that hippie could sue us. I've got to put an end to it." Two days later

Evelyn saw her turn onto Herb's dirt road. The Doberman started barking. Herb was eating a baloney sandwich at the kitchen table. He grabbed his hat and said, "I'm going out to talk to her." After that Evelyn only saw the woman walk on the county road. When the weather turned warm, she weeded and watered her garden with the baby in a backpack. She made it all look so easy. Wearing a floppy hat, she glided across their yard like she didn't have a care in the world. She sat in one of their chairs on the porch and read books. She probably didn't even watch TV. And she voted for a socialist Muslim. It didn't make sense, being like that and not looking like her life was a mess. Herb had worked hard and built Evelyn a brick house with a nice kitchen, and every ten years he bought her a new Cadillac. At night Herb quickly fell asleep as she lay awake. She thought about him. She hadn't had many choices. She was never a looker, and he was the only boy who took interest in her. She'd vowed, "Till death do us part."

Herb came to the table in a clean undershirt, Lee jeans, and slippers. Evelyn placed his plate of potatoes, steak, and peas in front of him. He cut into the steak before she sat down. "You overcooked the meat again," he said. She didn't say anything. A breeze blew her line of wind chimes hanging above the front porch. There was a wrought iron "Welcome" on the brick wall next to the door.

They ate in silence until he said, "Those bee boxes did their job: the fruit's coming in real nice. If the co-op pays $287 a ton again, we'll have another good year."

"That's good."

She got up for a glass of water. She placed a glass under the tap and watched the water until the Doberman started to bark. Here came the neighbor again. He's back? What the hell's he want? Water spilled over the rim of the glass onto her hand. Damn it. Herb cut into his baked potato and motioned with his knife for Evelyn to get the door. She wiped her hands on her apron and opened the door.

"Hello, you're Evelyn, right?" He smiled politely.

Evelyn was quiet. She stared at him. He had his hands in his pockets. Herb always said not to trust anyone who hid his hands.

"I'd like to talk with you about your dog."

"What about our dog?"

"It has been barking a lot at night, and it keeps us up."

"There are a lot of stray dogs around here. That's why it barks. I've called the pound about the strays, but they won't do anything about them. It's not our fault our dog barks at them. Maybe you should call the county."

"I understand your dog wanting to protect your property, but it often barks for hours late at night."

The neighbor's tone was not rude. Evelyn stared at him, her mouth downturned. The Doberman stopped barking.

"Tell that socialist to get off our porch," Herb said, still at the table.

The neighbor didn't react to Herb's comment, and neither did Evelyn. She put her arms on her hips. "What do you want me to do about it?"

"Pardon?"

"The dog, you were just complaining about our dog."

"Ma'am, I came here wanting to work this out as neighbors."

"Well you have a problem."

"What problem?"

"You wouldn't be here if you didn't have a problem, would you?" She heard herself sound like Herb. She stared at the neighbor coldly.

"We'd like the barking to stop. Actually, some barking is okay, but when it becomes incessant, it keeps us awake."

"So what do you want me to do, kill the dog?"

He placed his hand over his heart and shook his head. "I'm not asking you to kill your dog."

"Then what do you want me to do?"

"We would like if it didn't bark so much. It keeps us awake for hours, and we have a baby."

"Doesn't your baby keep you up at night?"

The neighbor paused. "Yes, but I'm sure you understand that that's different."

"Different my foot," Herb said.

Evelyn folded her arms. "No, I don't understand. We don't have children."

"Oh." He paused. "Anyway, can you please quiet your dog at night?"

"How? How am I supposed to quiet it down?"

"I don't know, ma'am. It's not my dog."

"Well I don't know either."

They stared at each other. Evelyn hadn't talked with anyone but Herb for awhile. Since her bridge group had stopped meeting for the summer, she'd been cooped up at home, knitting her friends' grandchildren sweaters, cleaning the house, doing the wash and the cooking, gardening some, and listening to Herb. He didn't like to have people over. Talking to the neighbor as the sun lowered into the trees, Evelyn felt an odd sense of satisfaction.

"So what do you want me to do about it?" she asked.

The neighbor took a deep breath and exhaled and started again in the same polite tone. "Okay, how would you like it if we had a dog that was keeping you up at night?"

"The dog's barking doesn't bother us."

"But what if we had a dog and it did?"

"But *we* have the dog, and it's not bothering us."

The neighbor paused. "I don't want to have to call the police over this."

"Now he's going to call the police. Some neighbor," Herb said.

"That wouldn't be the neighborly thing to do, would it?" Evelyn said.

"This conversation doesn't seem to be going anywhere."

"No, it doesn't."

"Okay then," he said and walked away, setting off the Doberman.

She understood that he'd call the police on them. They'd always stayed away from liberals, didn't like their protesting the American way. She was surprised by his resolve. She thought he'd just want to talk about his feelings with her. She had to admit, she was impressed by his backbone. She wondered if his wife was like that.

Evelyn tiptoed down the walkway. She watched him walk down their driveway past the John Deere tractor and Chevy truck, up the road, and across into his house. The Doberman barked the whole time and still barked even though the neighbor was out of sight. Evelyn stared at the neighbor's house. The Doberman barked. She turned toward the dog. "Shut up! Just shut up!" The dog whined and lay down on the cement.

Evelyn went inside and cleared Herb's plate and hers too, which still held most of her supper. Herb was in his chair in the living room reading the paper.

"Good job, hon," he said through the newspaper. "You didn't let him push you around."

She turned and looked at him. The newspaper blocked his entire upper body. She didn't need his input. She knew how to talk to others without him. What'd he think, that she was his puppet? She saw her face on one of those hand puppets, Herb's hand working the mouth open shut, open shut. She dumped her food in the trash and filled the sink with soapy water, replaying the conversation with the neighbor in her head, hearing her remarks and picturing the man nearly pleading with her.

Herb said, "You gotta put people like that in their place, and you did. He won't come back over here."

She was surprised by the neighbor's manners. She thought he'd be one of those know-it-all educated types who like to talk down to working folks. She'd seen him pushing the stroller and had seen him through their kitchen window washing dishes. She saw him in their garage doing laundry. He probably cooked too. She saw him come home from work and kiss his wife in their doorway. She wondered if his wife had told him to do those things. Did she have any idea what wives like Evelyn went through? Evelyn knew she'd been difficult with the neighbor, but she couldn't stop herself from talking to him like that. He didn't seem like a bad guy. She pictured his face, stunned, after some of the things she'd said to him. His wife most likely never talked to him like that. She probably didn't have a mean bone in her body.

Evelyn remembered a man who'd come to their door peddling World Book Encyclopedias some 40 years before. He wore a seersucker suit. They stood on the porch in hot summer air. The man wiped his brow and thick neck as he opened his case to show her the gold-embossed books. She knew that Herb wouldn't let her buy encyclopedias, but she wondered what it would be like to know more about everything. She knew he only cared about making a sale, but she still listened to him. "Knowledge is power. This entire set's $79.99. Compare that to four years of college." She pictured herself being able to talk to people like she knew something. She felt excited. The salesman was still standing on the porch when Herb's tractor roared out of a nearby row of peaches. Herb drove the tractor with disking blades to the front of the barn, parked it, and walked toward their house. He stopped in front of them and looked for a long time at the man and his books. The man wiped some sweat from his forehead and said, "Hello, sir."

Herb turned toward Evelyn. "Dinner ready?"

She looked at Herb. "No."

He walked into the house.

Herb would never let her buy them. She turned toward the salesman. "Sorry, but I can't buy encyclopedias."

Something bothered her that night as she lay down to sleep. She knew Herb would always work hard and they'd be comfortable, but she knew that wouldn't be enough. She'd made a mistake.

Now she reached into the soapy water and moved the sponge over a plate, thinking about the conversation with the neighbor, going over the dialogue and hearing herself being difficult. She hadn't given the man a chance. But she wasn't able to stop herself. She placed the dishes in the rack. She thought of what the young Evelyn would have said to the neighbor. She would have at least apologized for keeping him and his wife and baby awake. Evelyn scrubbed the pan. The neighbor had been nice. If Herb had been in his shoes, he would have bawled out the people and threatened to shoot their dog. She heard the neighbor trying to reason with her and her shoving it all back in his face. She felt bad. She remembered herself in the mirror and saw that ugly image right in front of her.

Evelyn went to the cupboard and pulled down a jar of homemade peach jam. She turned it in her hands as she looked out the window. She'd take it over there tomorrow and apologize and promise to keep the dog quiet. Maybe she'd get to know them and would be able to spend time with the woman. She'd exchange recipes with her, even the one for her peach cobbler that took first place at the county fair. She'd help her in the garden and would offer to take care of their place when they went away on weekends, as they often did. She would allow her to walk down Herb's dirt road. She'd knit the baby a sweater. If the woman were open to it, Evelyn would help with the baby. She'd babysit and take it for walks to give her new friend a rest. And as the little girl got bigger, maybe she would wave at her and say, "Hi, Aunt Evelyn." Butterflies filled her stomach.

Herb moved the paper to his lap and said, "I've been talking to you, and you haven't said a word. What the hell's the matter with you?"

Evelyn didn't respond. She stared across the street, turning the jar of jam in her hands.

"Can't you hear me? What the hell's the matter with you?"

She swung around. "Shut up!" she said. "Just shut up!"

# KEVIN SINCLAIR

When I was a kid, Kevin Sinclair was my idol.

I'd see Kevin Sinclair at Mannie's, throwing around the football or skidding on his bike. He and Mannie were three years older than me. He wasn't husky like Mannie, but he looked strong, probably because he was great at sports. It seemed like he didn't have to try hard at anything. His body moved smooth, like a cheetah's. I'd say, "Hi, Kevin," and he'd give me an upward nod or say, "Hey" while looking away. That was enough to make me feel important.

Kevin's straight brown hair hung over his calm brown eyes. He'd flip it back with a quick jerk of his head while fielding a ground ball or talking to girls in the cafeteria or sitting on the bus with the window open, looking grown up. At night I'd lock myself in the bathroom and wet my hair to make it hang over my eyes, but it never stayed straight. I'd try to flip it back like Kevin Sinclair, but my curls just bounced like a girl's, and I wouldn't like looking at myself in the mirror because of it. My dad would bang on the door. "What the hell are you doing in there all the time?"

"Leave the boy alone, Ron," my mom would say from the kitchen.

"I'm not talking to you, so keep quiet."

I liked that my mom would stick up for me, but I was scared that my dad would push her against the wall again. The one time he did it, all I did was stand there and cry. The day after that happened my mom said, "Why didn't you do something?" I didn't know what to say, so I didn't say anything.

*

Ray was my best friend. We had Mrs. Deadder for second grade. It was late May. Outside the blacktop broiled. Inside our square fan hummed. Flopped over, we rested our heads on our desks and wrote between the big lines. Out of nowhere twelve fifth graders paraded in with Mr. Jacobs, our principal who wore a tie and had long sideburns and knew every kid's name in the school. Having those big kids in our room woke us up like a kung-fu movie. They lined up in the front of the room. Kevin Sinclair was at the far end, leaning against the chalkboard. He stared down at the ground like he didn't care about anything.

"Class," Mrs. Deadder began, "Mr. Jacobs is here with some very important students."

"Good afternoon boys and girls. I'm here with a group of fifth graders running for school Treasurer, Secretary, Vice President, and President. They are here to share their political speeches with you so you will know how to vote this Friday for our school elections, so listen carefully."

They all looked so big, towering over our little desks with their feathered hair, holding their speeches written in cursive. Kevin Sinclair wasn't holding a speech. All of them looked nervous but not Kevin Sinclair.

"Go ahead and start us off, Steve," Mr. Jacobs said with a nod.

A boy stood up straight and read from his sheet of paper. "My name is Steve Pierce, and I'm running for Treasurer. As Treasurer I'll take care of all the money at Oakfield, and I'll try to make recess longer and get better food in the cafeteria. So this Friday, vote for Steve Pierce for Treasurer. Thank you."

I didn't know what a Treasurer was or what one did, but more recess was a good idea, and so was better food. I'd vote for him. Ray and I looked at each other and nodded. But when the next Treasurer person—Kathy Shaw—stood up straight and read her speech, she mentioned money and recess and cafeteria food too, so I got confused. Then other fifth graders mentioned recess and cafeteria food, and soon our heads rested on our desks, and the heat covered us like a blanket.

All this time Kevin Sinclair was leaning against the chalkboard, still looking down at the ground. When it was finally his turn, he pushed off the board and raised his hand. "I'm Kevin Sinclair, and if I'm elected President of Oakfield Elementary School, I'll put chocolate milk in all the drinking fountains."

Our heads sprang up. Fat Timmy Tompkins said, "Chocolate milk in the *drinking fountains!*" We screamed and looked around at each other. I pictured cold chocolate milk flowing out of the old metal fountains and felt it silky on my lips and going down my throat one sweet slurp at a time.

"It will be there whenever we want it!" Timmy said.

"And we won't have to pay five cents extra for chocolate milk!" Ray said.

"And we'll be able to take some home in our thermoses!" I added. My dad never let my mom buy chocolate milk. It was too expensive, like those canned juices that some kids brought to school.

Mr. Jacobs said, "Thank you for listening, boys and girls." He started toward the door with the big kids behind him. When Kevin Sinclair passed my desk, he gave me one of his upward nods, and firecrackers went off in my chest. I looked at the other boys, and they all smiled. We couldn't wait to vote.

Friday afternoon Mr. Jacobs announced the winners. "Kevin Sinclair will be Oakfield's next Student Body President." We all howled and ran around the playground punching yellow tetherballs.

*

It was the longest summer of my life. Every week I went to the liquor store where my dad worked. I helped my dad stock shelves, and I snuck candy and sat in front of a rusty fan. I'd stand in front of the cold box and look at the brown and white chocolate milk cartons. The cows on them were smiling. At home I kept clear of my mom when she got overloaded at work and had to bring home piles of pants to hem. Once in a while my dad and I watched baseball together. Sometimes when Ray wasn't on fishing trips with his dad and brother, we played on his homemade slip-n-slide. All of our conversations led to the chocolate milk and how it would taste after playing kickball or dodge ball or after walking out of the boys' bathroom and taking a sip just because it was there.

One time his dad heard us talking. "Don't be silly, boys. Schools can't put chocolate milk in drinking fountains." Neither Ray nor I said anything. Ray's dad didn't know Kevin Sinclair. I didn't risk telling my dad. He wouldn't understand either. I made a calendar and crossed out days until September 15th. The summer crawled across hot pavement like a snail.

*

The first day of school finally arrived. Wearing my new Levis, I raced to school on my bike, bag lunch dangling from my handlebars. Ray was there. So was Timmy Tompkins, with his new velour shirt and shiny lunch box. Other kids were already there too, spread out along the yellow boundary line that couldn't be crossed until the bell rang at 8:10. Ray and I nudged our way up to the front. Two sets of drinking fountains hung off the wall straight ahead.

The school secretary walked out of the office toward the teachers' room. Timmy yelled, "Mrs. Frankle, can we cross the line early to get some chocolate milk?"

"You know that you can't cross the line until 8:10, boys and girls." Then she was called into the teachers' room by Mrs. Brown, the kindergarten teacher with bad breath.

"Figures," Timmy said.

More kids ran up. Now the sidewalk was packed. Timmy yelled, "Quit pushin'!" Nobody listened. "When's that thing gonna ring?" Timmy said. A second later the metal bell clanged, and we were sprinting. Ray and I got to the nearest fountain first. I took a deep breath and stretched my lips, ready to taste the smooth chocolate milk. Just as I turned the handle, Timmy yelled from another fountain, "It's *water!*" And then plain water splashed my lips. Other kids at other drinking fountains yelled, "It's *water!* It's *water!*" I stood up straight and stared at the water fountain. I turned the knob again. Water. The more water I watched flow, the more it felt like my insides were draining out of me.

We stood in line outside of our classrooms and shared possible reasons for this mistake.

"They must still be working on it," I said.

"Maybe there's a problem with the pipes," Ray said.

"Maybe it will be ready for lunch," Timmy said.

At first recess we checked again. Only water arched from the spouts. It was the same at lunch and after school. A group of third graders came to me. "You gotta find out what happened."

"Why me?"

"Because you live near Mannie, and he's friends with Kevin Sinclair."

I was nervous, but I liked that I'd be the one to talk to him.

\*

I rode my bike past Mannie's. Kevin Sinclair was there. He and Mannie were sitting on his porch looking at baseball cards. My palms were sweaty. I kept riding by, thinking about what I'd say. I practiced saying it out loud a couple of times. Finally I stopped in front of Mannie's house and straddled my bike. "Hey, Kevin, what happened to the chocolate milk?"

He kept flipping through his cards. "They wouldn't let me do it." That's all he said. Then he pulled a card from his stack and turned to Mannie. "Check out this Joe Morgan card." He looked through more cards, his head still down, his hair hanging over his eyes. I stood there for a while, but Kevin Sinclair still didn't look up at me. Mannie's orange cat meowed and rubbed up against my leg. Mannie said, "Joe Morgan's cool." When I rode off, Kevin was handing Mannie a George Foster card. He still didn't look up. I rode home slow, feeling worse than I did when I'd watched only water pour from the fountain. The sidewalk rolled under my bike like water.

That night at dinner my mom surprised me with my favorite food: a beanie weenie TV dinner. She smiled proudly as she pulled it out of the oven and peeled back the foil top. I just stared at it, seeing Kevin Sinclair on Mannie's porch looking at his stupid baseball cards. I heard him say, "They wouldn't let me do it." He didn't really care.

My mom spread butter on her potato. My dad cut into his steak. "What's wrong, honey?" my mom asked. "That's your favorite."

"Kevin Sinclair didn't put chocolate milk in the drinking fountains."

"Huh?"

"Kevin Sinclair, Mannie's friend, said that he'd put chocolate milk in the drinking fountains if he became school President, but he didn't because he said they wouldn't let him do it."

My dad chuckled. "*Chocolate milk in the drinking fountains*—that's the best one I've heard in a long time. Smart kid. He'll probably be in the White House someday." He shook a bottle of the Thousand Island dressing and poured some on his salad. "Don't cry about it. That boy just knew what to say, like any politician." He screwed the white top on the bottle and looked at me.

I turned to my mom. She nodded as if it was the most obvious thing in the world.

Their forks and knives scraped against their plates, and they went on eating like it wasn't a big deal. I looked down at my food. I shouldn't have told them. I knew they wouldn't understand. I was talking about Kevin Sinclair. I wasn't talking about just anybody. I was talking about Kevin Sinclair.

# BRIDE FINDER

Sam Tootle awoke one morning ready to find his bride. He'd lived in a Zairian village for two months. *Mamas* pounded dried manioc in wooden mortars throughout the village. He walked through the village on dirt paths, following the drumming of pounding pestles that led him to the edges of parcels with mud huts and roaming chickens and goats. Sam only stopped at the edges of lots where teenage girls were pounding. They raised long pestles with both hands, rocked forward, and crashed them into mortars, as he imagined women in Africa had done for centuries. Seeing this deep history added more meaning to his volunteer work in Zaire. The pounding was so primal, so native, so wild. It stirred a visceral pang in his gut that he had first felt in high school geography, when he saw African girls in a National Geographic film carrying buckets of water on their heads, their lithe bodies glistening with sweat, their short hair smoothly covering their perfectly round heads, their big dark eyes looking into the camera, occasionally blinking like models in a mascara commercial.

*

Tata Mukali was snooping around his family's parcel, looking under fallen palm fronds, alongside their mud hut, and next to a papaya tree for the daily egg his hen laid. The old widow next door yelled, "Hey Mukali, I went to my son's for some peanuts and saw the *mundele* staring at girls pounding manioc. He sure likes the young ones."

"Oh!" he said and hurried inside.

He'd had his eye on Sam since his arrival, but he could never lure him to his family's house because the *mundele* was always working. Tata Mukali put on a clean shirt, made sure his big feet were clean, and chewed on the end of a soft stick to brush his teeth. His daughter Pama was pounding away with her mother, Mama Dinga.

He flung open the flimsy door and hurried out, his long legs flying forward.

Mama Dinga looked at him. "Where are you going this early looking so good?"

Tata Mukali waved her off and scurried away, taking big steps and leaning forward. He snaked around mud huts, kicking chickens and goats along the way. He saw the stocky *mundele* watching a girl pounding manioc and sweating in the tropical heat. Her short father stood next to him. "Uh oh," Tata Mukali said and started to run.

The girl thrust her hips to raise the big piece of wood. Her father stood next to Sam with his arm around Sam, who stared at the girl. Her batik wrapped tightly around her small hips, her budding breasts didn't move under her t-shirt, her chocolate skin was silky nice. She was similar to the girls he'd seen in the film nine years before. She just might do.

Tata Mukali ran up. He was breathing fast "*Monsieur...*I... am—"

The girl's father waved his hand at him. "*Excusez-moi*, Tata Mukali, but *I* was talking with the *monsieur*."

The two villagers began to banter, but Sam didn't pay attention to any of it. The girl pounded and rocked and pounded, thrusting the wood with such downward force—it was so primal, so sensual.

The girl's father pulled on Sam's white t-shirt. "Come, come, let's have some palm wine."

Tata Mukali pulled on Sam's arm. "I have *the* girl for you. She's much more beautiful than this one."

Sam adjusted his glasses. His little eyes widened. "Yeah?"

Tata Mukali closed his eyes and nodded. "Yes."

"Don't listen to him, *Monsieur*. You can have my daughter right *now.*" The short man grabbed Sam's arm and pointed at the girl. "Look at her—she is yours right now."

Tata Mukali stepped in front of Sam to block his view. "But my daughter is more beautiful."

"She is?" Sam asked.

The girl's father shoved Tata Mukali. "You thief, stop trying to steal him from me. Shame on you."

Tata Mukali pulled back his fist. "Shut up, pygmy."

The other man flinched.

"Come see her," Tata Mukali said and led Sam away.

Sam walked with his hands in his pockets. Tata Mukali towered over him and flopped a long arm over a shoulder.

"How old is your daughter?"

"Fourteen."

"Really?" Sam began to think about fourteen-year-old girls— on the border between childhood and adolescence, inexperienced and curious about the ways of the world, smooth skin covering a developing body. Between academic years at Calvin College, Sam had returned home in May to Olivia, North Dakota, to work on the family hog farm. He'd park across from Olivia High to watch young high school girls. Not the juniors and seniors who held themselves like women, but the freshmen and sophomores—the ones whose bodies were starting to form. The ones who still needed to depend on an adult. He knew that he couldn't pursue one of them because American society didn't understand the natural connection between a man and a girl. Nor did he want to pursue girls in Olivia. They weren't African.

Mukali's mud hut was up ahead. As they walked Sam looked down at the ground. He thought about the body of a fourteen-year-old African girl. Caressing her back, still sweaty after pounding manioc.

"*Monsieur*, I know that you probably wish that she were thirteen, or even twelve, but you must know that she has never left my sight. She is pure."

They were now at the edge of Tata Mukali's parcel. Sam hadn't looked up. He was still daydreaming about stroking a fourteen-year-old African body. He felt manly.

Pama was alone outside, pounding the manioc like a steady jack hammer.

Tata Mukali glanced at him again, saw that same blank look on his face, and began to panic. "*Monsieur*, I cannot lower the years of my daughter, but I can lower the amount that you will need to pay me."

Pay? Sam thought.

"Look at her." Tata Mukali pointed at Pama fifteen meters away, pounding manioc, lifting, thrusting, then grinding the wood into the deep mortar. "She is in her prime."

Sam was stunned. The other girl's body was as petite and undeveloped as this one's, but this one had high cheek bones, round eyes, and slender fingers. This one embodied his image of a beautiful African native girl. This was her. She was the one. Sam fixed a stare on Tata Mukali.

"How much?"

"You will need to give me palm wine once a month for three months and—"

"How much does palm wine cost?"

"Twenty five Zaires per calabash."

Sam thought, 100 Zaires = 1 U.S dollar, so roughly 25 cents a calabash. Cheap. He looked at Tata Mukali and nodded.

Tata Mukali smiled. "The first time you bring me palm wine, you will need to bring three chickens. A chicken costs 100 Zaires."

So $3 total for the chickens + .25 cents = $3.25. Still cheap. He nodded.

"The second time you bring palm wine, you must bring a goat, which costs 2,000 Zaires."

2,000 Zaires = $20. Very good.

Sam nodded. Tata Mukali patted Sam on the back. "And the third time you bring me palm wine, you must bring a cow—5,000 Zaires—and you must give me 5,000 Zaires.

Okay, so $100 + $20 + $3=$123 + .75 for the palm wine totals $123.75. Unbelievable bargain. Sam looked down and shook his head in disbelief.

Tata Mukali's eyes widened. "Is my price too high, *Monsieur*?
"Is that how much you want?"
"If the cow and 5,000 Zaires is too much, how about the cow and 3,000 Zaires? Yes, 3,000 Zaires is better."
$123.75 - $20 = $103.75!
"*Monsieur*, I know it is a lot of money, but—"
"That will be fine." They shook hands.
Tata Mukali smiled big and wrapped his arm around Sam. "Good, now let's go meet my daughter."

*

Each of the two months Sam had been at post, he'd written letters home. He'd always written home—from summer Scout camps and from college. He thought it showed his loyalty toward his parents and older brother, even though they weren't letter-writers and didn't understand why Sam wanted to go to Africa.

In his first letter, he wrote that his village consisted of mud-stick houses sitting on rock-hard earth, and that it had few palm trees because it was very dry there. It hadn't rained in many months, and villagers feared a drought. But the lack of rain meant very little malaria. He wrote that his hut was close to the village well. It had one main room with a table in the center and a bed in the corner. He told them that his place had glassless windows that looked out at sandy savannah. He wrote that he didn't open the shutters because he didn't want others knowing what he had, and thought that it would cut down on all the flies.

He devoted his second letter to his animal husbandry work— that he'd built a demonstration rabbit hutch and pig corral and that the village men had requested his help in building their own. He said that though he was busy working with villagers throughout the day, the work couldn't compare with that on the family hog farm. At home he had either worked alone or with his dad and brother. Sam worked as hard as they did at jobs like feeding and castrating the pigs and shoveling their stalls, but he didn't have their mechanical skills. He had trouble changing oil, much less adjusting a carburetor or replacing a fan belt, or welding a cage. His father and brother first called him "useless," and then "useless college boy," and finally "useless college grad." The Zairians thought otherwise of Sam. They thanked him generously and paid him with praise and *fufu* lunches, which built his confidence. Sam didn't include this information in his letter—his father would view him as a braggart. Nor did he write immediately after becoming engaged.

*

After agreeing on a price, Sam and Tata Mukali walked toward the family hut. Sam watched Pama. She looked at him once but mainly looked into the mortar. Mama Dinga walked out of the hut holding a large pot for the manioc flour. She didn't notice her husband and the *mundele*.

Bulu, their fourteen-year-old son, crutched out of the hut behind her. He wore shorts, and his twisted leg and bulbous foot flopped forward, sometimes hitting the carved wooden crutch. Sam recognized polio. He thought back to his grandfather who had battled the disease. He used to struggle with his cane, especially when he went up stairs. Sam felt sorry for him, but his grandfather wasn't the type to want sympathy. When Sam was a kid, he still worked around the farm, moving feed with the tractor or running for parts in his Ford F-150. Sam often went with him. Once on their way to the feed store, he pulled over alongside a corn field, and said, "Don't trap yourself on a farm like your father did." Sam listened and promised himself that he wouldn't end up like his father.

Sam wasn't bothered by Bulu's shriveled foot that hooked inward, but the dead, bloody toenail on the boy's big toe twisted his stomach. All Peace Corps Volunteers had their phobias: for some it was getting malaria; for others, eating rats or grubs; for others, having a snake slither under their mosquito net and into their bed. For Sam, it was anything involving blood. He could eat a bologna sandwich in the middle of a pen full of pig shit, but if he nicked his face with a razor, he had to sit down.

Tata Mukali didn't know why Sam had stopped. He saw Sam looking ill. Tata Mukali ran at his son waving his arms. "Get inside! Get! Get!"

Bulu dropped his crutch and hopped on his good leg toward the door until Mama Dinga ran to him. "Don't yell at him, Mukali. What's wrong with you?" Then she saw Sam. She swatted Tata Mukali on the arm.

Embarrassed, he looked at Sam. "Don't worry, *Monsieur*, there's no problem."

Sam nodded. He looked at Pama's sweat-covered body and the image of the boy's bloody toenail began to fade. Sam watched Pama rock, pound, and grind. There was his beautiful African girl, finally in the flesh, right in front of him. He wanted to reach for her. Mama Dinga saw Sam groping her daughter with his eyes. She ran to Pama, grabbed her arm, and yanked her toward the house. The pestle got caught on the lip and hit the ground, shooting out white manioc flour. Pama looked back with alarm, but Mama Dinga didn't. She pulled Pama toward the house. Before they reached the door, Tata Mukali grabbed Pama's other arm and stopped them.

"Dinga, let go of her. The girl must stay outside with me. I'm doing this for her."

Mama Dinga let go of Pama and marched toward Sam waving the big pot at him. "*Mundele*, if you think you're going to get my daughter—"

Sam adjusted his glasses, raised his hands in the air, and took a couple steps backward. Before Mama Dinga reached him, Tata Mukali grabbed the pot and stepped in front of her. "Enough."

"Are you blind, Mukali? He looks at our daughter with his rodent eyes like she's the first girl he's ever seen." She shook her head. "My God, do you want him to give palm wine and make your daughter a marked woman? You'll ruin her."

"What do you know?"

"Have you forgotten about Kalaki's daughter? That smooth talker—Dongo was his name—gave palm wine then disappeared to Kinshasa. You don't see any men looking at her now, do you? What are you thinking?" Mama Dinga slapped him upside the head and pulled Pama into the hut.

"*Excusez-moi, Monsieur.* I will fix things, and we will talk tomorrow," Tata Mukali said.

Sam nodded.

Tata Mukali went inside. Sam moved close to the mud hut and listened.

"Dinga, it's Pama's way to riches. Don't you want your daughter to have a good life?"

Sam smiled and walked away. On his way home he saw other girls, probably also Pama's age. They weren't as pretty, but he couldn't stop himself from looking.

*

The next day Mama Dinga knocked on Sam's door before the *mamas* started to pound manioc. Sam jumped out of bed and opened the door. The entire family was standing there. Tata Mukali stepped forward. "I'm sorry that we're here so early, *Monsieur*, but she insisted."

Mama Dinga walked right in. The others followed. Tata Mukali gave Sam an apologetic look. Pama looked straight ahead. Bulu crutched in, leaving divots in Sam's dirt floor. The boy looked embarrassed. "Don't worry about that, Bulu," Sam said.

"You listen, *mundele*," Mama Dinga said. "Mukali made me agree to this marriage, so now I have to cook for you. I don't want to because I don't like you and your eyes that are like a village rat's, but I'll cook enough for you, and Pama will help you, and Bulu will clean your house every day when you're eating lunch at our house."

A rooster crowed from afar. Others joined in.

"I'd like Bulu to visit as much as he wants, but he doesn't have to work."

"He's crippled, but he can still work."

Sam adjusted his glasses. "But—"

"No, no, that's what Bulu will do." She nodded once.

Sam wasn't going to argue with his future mother-in-law.

"We'll start all this tomorrow. Let's go," she said. They filed out.

"Thank you," Sam said.

Walking away she shook her head and mumbled to herself, "I have to hold on to something. It's bad enough that I've lost her to that *Sam*. What kind of man goes by *Sam*? And *Tootle*—sounds like a sick chicken. One sick child is bad enough, no need for another, and one from a place with people like him, ones you can't trust. Ones that look at girls like they're fresh beef."

*

Sam taught Pama how to fold his 38-inch-waist Levis with the 30-inch inseam. He liked a crease down the middle, so he made her practice lining up the seams. They stood next to the table. He looked at Pama's petite hips sealed in her batik wrap and at her budding breasts. He glanced at Pama's soft short hair and high cheek bones and felt proud and excited. She folded the jeans and looked up at him.

He'd always wanted to see such a native woman but didn't have any luck in Olivia or at college in Grand Rapids. Sam knew that hardly anyone from North Dakota ever applied to the Peace Corps. He was able to choose his continent and country. When Sam had arrived at post, he studied the daughters of his livestock farmers. They were young enough, but they weren't quite right. One had arms like a man, another filed teeth, and another walked like an egret. After two months, he realized that he had to be more aggressive, had to search her out. Pama was perfect.

"Good," Sam said to Pama after she folded his third pair of jeans. "Now fold all these two more times. Then I'll show you how to fold my shirts."

"Is this how I'll fold your clothes when we get to America?"

"Yes." He squeezed her hand.

He went to his dresser and pulled out a stack of white t-shirts that read "Calvin College" or "CC."

Pama finished her task and turned toward Sam. He peeled a shirt off the stack. "There's a perfect way to fold shirts." He demonstrated the standard way to fold a t-shirt and stepped back. Pama took over. It reminded him of watching his mother fold his father's t-shirts. Sam had sent a third letter home almost a month before. They must have received it. Sam wondered about his parents' reaction to his engagement.

There was a bang at the door.

"It must be Bulu," Sam said.

He opened the door. "Hey, there he is," Sam said and high-fived Bulu.

The boy hobbled inside, his shriveled up left leg flopping forward as he crutched. Bulu carried a palm frond in his free hand. "Is there anything special that you want me to do, Sam?"

"No. This place is still clean from yesterday. Just rest if you want."

Pama picked up the clothes and glided over to Sam's bed in the corner of the room. Sam moved aside to let Pama place the wooden chairs on the table. Bulu started to sweep the dirt floor with the palm frond. "Bon appetit," he said, and Sam and Pama left.

Sam walked the fifty meters to eat his *fufu* lunch in the shade of the family's hut while Pama went to fetch rationed water from the low well. Mama Dinga hardly said a word to Sam. It bothered him. Since he'd been engaged, he'd built the family a double level hutch and filled it with rabbits. He'd also built a large corral and stocked it with pigs. Pama had brought him water as he worked. Bulu sat nearby and kept him company. Mama Dinga never acknowledged Sam's work. It ate away at him. Some nights he lay awake knowing that she saw through him. She knew what he was up to with young girls. He was careful not to look at other girls in the village, but he always snuck in a peek at their breasts when they were carrying buckets of water on their heads and at their rears when they were hoeing a field. He wondered if she had seen him looking.

Like every day over the past month, while Sam and Pama were gone, Bulu explored Sam's dresser. He turned pages of books that he didn't know were on African history, looked underneath all the t-shirts and jeans, pulled out the same pictures of Sam standing with three other people who looked like him—his parents and older brother. In the photo the family was standing next to a truck with huge hogs in the background. Bulu had told his mother about this picture. She had remarked, "They are all fat like him? And they have an auto *and* so many pigs? They are very rich. Maybe your father is right to make Pama marry this *mundele*. But keep looking through his things. He must be hiding something."

"I don't want to. I like Sam."

She clenched his arm. "You keep looking. You can never trust a *mundele*. Look what the Belgians did to us."

Bulu had kept looking, but every day he found the same things, some that puzzled him. He didn't understand why Sam used a brush for his teeth when a stick could do the same job. He wondered why Sam had white shirts—white is hard to clean and uses too much soap. And he was completely baffled by Sam's small red knife that couldn't even skin a rabbit. But when it came to Sam's big socks, even though they were white, Bulu fell in love: only the rich could afford socks. Some villagers wore shoes to funerals, but nobody had socks. The first time Bulu had seen Sam, he noticed his socks and wondered what they felt like. He thought having one on his bad foot would feel nice, especially when it bashed against the crutch. Every day after Sam and Pama left he slipped one on. He knew when to put it away: long before Sam reached his hut, the kids next door always yelled, "Hey *mundele!*" That day Bulu found nothing new. There wasn't anything new to find, but he liked wearing a sock every day, so he followed his mother's orders.

*

During that first month of the engagement, Sam had given the first palm wine. When Sam arrived at his hut with a calabash of palm wine and three chickens, Tata Mukali set the chickens down to roam. "The others are away. We need our time." He and Sam sat in the shade of the hut and drank.

Tata Mukali talked about growing up under Belgian rule, and learning how to make furniture, and about living in a sandy area that hardly saw rain. He liked that Sam listened and asked him questions about his life, but he was most pleased that his future son-in-law could drink.

Back home, Sam's father and brother would share a twelve-pack of Ham's after a day of work, and Sam would maybe drink a beer to cool off. The few times in college that he'd filled his big gut with alcohol, he hardly felt it. Sam and Tata Mukali talked and lazily passed the calabash back and forth until it was empty. Tata Mukali slurred through his last story before leaning back on his elbows and passing out. Sam threw him over his shoulder and carried him inside, Tata Mukali's knuckles nearly dragging on the ground. Sam put him in his bed and walked home happy. He was one step closer to realizing his bridal fantasy.

*

While driving through Sam's village, Margie, the Assistant Peace Corps Director, dropped off his mail—one aerogram from home. He quickly ducked inside and opened the letter.

Dear Sam,

Father and I were very surprised by your news. We thought you were there to help those people, not marry one of them. If you love Palm Tree then I will accept her. There aren't any colored people around here, so we're not sure she will like Olivia. I'm pleased that you're helping the boy with polio. Grandpa Harvey would be proud.

Dad had to get a few stitches last week. He was cutting a limb from the maple tree and the chainsaw kicked back and nicked his cheek. He bled real bad. You would've fainted.

The hogs are doing fine. None have froze and the price of pork looks good. Your brother's taken over the sow pens, which is fine with dad. They're both fine.

Be safe,
Mom

Sam dropped the letter on the table. He imagined his father drinking Ham's beer and hollering because his son was to marry a *colored*. He knew that his mother and brother felt the same way. His mother hadn't written anything about his father and brother accepting Pama. When he finished his service in Zaire, he and Pama would not live in Olivia. They would start their own life.

\*

The day before Sam was to give the second calabash of palm wine and the goat, Bulu was doing his daily sweep and snoop. Sam had bought the goat and tied it to a post outside his door. Like every other day, Bulu swept and then slid a big cushy white sock on his bad leg. Bored, he lay down on Sam's bed and fell asleep.

Bulu dreamed that he was crutching through the village in a sock that nearly reached his knee. All the villagers lined the road and clapped. His parents beamed, and his father nodded at him with approval, making Bulu feel ten feet tall. Then from somewhere behind all of the clapping, Bulu heard, "Hey *mundele!*" But the clapping got louder, and some people even yelled, "You're so handsome, Bulu!" He crutched along and waved to everybody, but he still heard, "Hey *mundele!*" Then he heard something else, closer. Bulu bolted upright, his eyes bulging.

Sam was outside with his hand on the door latch. The goat nibbled on his shoe lace. Sam said, "No!" He pushed it away. Bulu flew off the bed. The goat went for Sam's other shoe, and Sam pushed it away again, giving Bulu enough time to smooth out the bed, pull off the sock, and throw it into the dresser. But in the process he tore off his dead toenail, and his toe was bleeding all over the place when Sam opened the door.

"Hey, Bulu. How's it— " Sam saw Bulu's foot dripping blood. He sat at the table and took big breaths and tried to ignore the nausea.

"Sorry, Sam. I hurt myself. I must go home." Bulu hurried out.

Sam caught his breath and walked outside. Bulu was nearly at his home. Sam jogged toward him. Mama Dinga was outside.

"Are you okay, Bulu?" Sam said.

"I'll be fine."

"What happened to your foot?" Mama Dinga asked.

"Nothing."

"So what's the problem?" she asked Sam.

"He bled on my floor."

"Oh, is that all?" She marched to Sam's hut. He followed but stopped when she went inside. "What's wrong with you?"

"I don't like blood."

She shook her head and mumbled something about him being ridiculous. She poured some water on the spots and swept them with her foot. Finished, she marched away.

Sam crept inside looking for any signs of blood.

*

Sam woke early, took a bucket bath, and was pulling on a sock when his big toe hit something sharp and hard. He pulled off the sock and saw a blood spot. "Blood?" He grew queasy. He looked at his foot and didn't see blood. He turned the sock inside out. The crusty toenail fell into his lap. He jumped like it was a black mamba.

Mama Dinga and Pama were cooking manioc on open fire when Sam walked up holding out the sock.

"You're too early," Mama Dinga said, not looking at him. She shook her head. "Come back when breakfast is ready."

"I'm here for Bulu."

"He's still asleep. What do you want?"

Sam turned over the sock and pointed. "I think that's Bulu's blood."

"How do you know?"

"His toenail fell out of it."

"You might be right, *mundele*. His toenail *was* missing yesterday."

She walked toward the house, wooden spoon in hand.

"Bulu, get out here."

"No."

"Bulu! I'll beat you out of there if—"

The door opened and Bulu crept out.

"Were you wearing the *mundele's* sock?"

"I didn't mean—"

She whacked his foot with the spoon.

"Ooowww!"

"Now apologize to him."

Bulu wouldn't look at Sam.

She raised her spoon. "Bulu, you—"

"*You* apologize to him. You're the one who told me to go through his things every day."

Mama Dinga blushed. Sam's mouth dropped open.

She rushed to him and grabbed his arm. "I did it for my daughter, to make sure you were good for her." Mama Dinga looked at Sam.

Sam turned and walked home smiling. Now he had the upper hand.

An hour later the entire family knocked at Sam's hut. Mama Dinga and Bulu hung their heads. "My wife has something to say to you," Tata Mukali said.

"I'm sorry."

"It's all right," Sam said.

"Really?" she said.

"Yes. You're being a responsible mother."

Mama Dinga smiled proudly.

"So Bulu, you like my socks?"

"Yes."

Sam pulled a pair from his back pocket and handed them to him. "These are for you."

"Thank you, Sam!"

Everybody smiled, but Sam smiled the most.

*

Sam returned the following day with the palm wine and tethered goat. *Fufu*, corn, and peanuts covered a table outside. Tata Mukali shook Sam's hand and tied the goat to a post. They shared some palm wine and talked. The door to the hut opened. Pama emerged in new batik. Mama Dinga was behind her. She took Pama's hand and gave it to Sam. Mama Dinga wrapped her hands around theirs and looked at Sam. "I'm sorry that I was mistaken about you." Tata Mukali smiled proudly. The girl looked down at the ground. Sam finally felt welcomed.

They all sat down together and started to eat with their hands, first pulling off wads of *fufu* and scooping up boiled corn and peanuts and dabbing it all with *pili pili* pepper sauce. Half way through the meal the wind picked up, and dark clouds rolled over the horizon toward them. "Hallelujah," Mama Dinga said. Dust devils raced about the village, lifting loose savannah grass into the sky. Mama Dinga took in the food, Tata Mukali carried the calabash, and Sam and Pama walked hand-in-hand alongside Bulu. They sat inside, excited. The goat and the chickens huddled up against the hut.

Monster drops bounced off the hard earth, and water puddled in low areas. Thunder exploded and lightning flashed, illuminating the sky and the inside of the hut through the rest of the afternoon and into the night. Rain fell from all directions. Water rushed down paths, roads, rat trails, house posts, backs of cows, and down sides of huts. The wind blew harder. Loose thatch flew from roofs. Villagers howled over braying goats, squealing pigs, and crying babies. Some people knelt in their huts and prayed for it to stop. Sam stayed with the family.

Mud walls of huts grew soft and oozed out of their stick frames. Latrines filled and excrement floated into yards. More thunder cracked and lightning burst and people cried throughout the village as they huddled in dark corners of their homes and saw more destruction every time lightning flashed.

Water soaked through layers of thatch until roofs were like loaded sponges and began to leak. Everything became soaked— clothes, blankets, hair.

Through all the misery, Sam kept saying, "We'll get through this.

Everything will be fine." Tata Mukali looked at Sam nervously. Sam knew that he'd become the family's rock. He wished that his father and brother could see him now.

Nearly an entire wall had washed away when lightning hit the roof. A blue band of electricity singed the wet thatch, and parts of the roof started falling down upon them. Sam threw Bulu over his shoulder, grabbed Pama's hand, and yelled, "Come on!" They ran through muck to reach Sam's home.

His roof was leaking, but his walls were intact. The group sat on his wet mattress, shivering, and holding on to each other until the rain stopped before dawn. Pama and her family fell asleep while Sam stayed up, proud of what he'd done. Before falling asleep, he wondered if his family back home would have been proud of him.

\*

When things were dry enough to repair, Sam led the charge. He worked on the family home from sunup to sundown, only stopping for lunch. He dug pits and used the dirt to make mud, filled in stick frames to replace walls, and spread a layer of manure-grass finish on the exterior walls. Tata Mukali gathered thatch from the fields. Once Sam finished the walls, they re-thatched the roof. Sam dug a new latrine, and Tata Mukali built a roof over it. Pama and Mama Dinga washed the men's clothes daily. Once the men finished the work on the home, they started to help neighbors rebuild their huts.

The family and other villagers thanked and praised Sam throughout, telling him that they had never seen anyone work as hard. An old widow wove him a small basket and gave it to Sam. "You're a good man." His father and brother wouldn't call him "useless" if they could see him.

After dinner one night, as Sam was talking about the work to be finished on neighbors' homes, Mama Dinga, Pama, and Bulu got up from the table and walked out into the night.

"Where are they going?" Sam asked.

"Let them be," Tata Mukali said and poured two cups of palm wine.

"You have been very good to us. I will not accept your money or a cow." He raised his plastic cup. "May this be the third palm wine."

Sam shook his father-in-law's hand, and they drank. Tata Mukali led Sam to his hut. Mama Dinga and Bulu were standing outside. Mama Dinga knocked on the door. A village elder holding a candle led Pama by the hand and positioned her next to Sam. The wedding ceremony was very short and did not include a kiss, but the two held hands and Sam couldn't stop smiling at Pama.

Mama Dinga hugged Sam. Bulu shook his hand. Tata Mukali opened the door and motioned for Sam to take Pama inside.

Lit candles glowed about the room. Pama sat on the bed with her head down. As Sam walked toward her, she looked up at him and smiled.

*

Sam loved waking up with his girl. He asked Pama to sleep naked, and most mornings he woke up before her to stare at her innocent face, her silky skin, and her smooth body with its dark nipples and small pubic patch. Pama pounded the manioc, washed his clothes, cooked the meals, and fetched the water. Sam liked to watch her work. He still watched other girls as they hoed or carried baskets of manioc tubers or buckets of water. He couldn't help himself. He was a man after all. Most nights Sam and Pama visited with Pama's family. Sam taught them how to play Spades. Sometimes other villagers stood around the family's table just to watch them hoot and laugh.

*

One morning, while Sam was looking at Pama's bare body, he heard a car engine in the distance. Before Sam could put on his shoes, Margie was pulling up to his hut in her red Land Cruiser.

"Sam! Are you here?"

He ran outside. Pama followed.

"Getting cozy with the natives, huh?"

"This is my wife."

"Well you picked the wrong time to get married—the State Department's evacuating us."

"What?"

"Military insurrection. Soldiers are killing foreigners. This country's gone to hell."

Mama Dinga and Tata Mukali ran up. Bulu crutched toward

them.

"I need to drop you and some other volunteers off at the nearest airstrip before heading out to another area. Grab what you want to take home."

"Now?"

Margie jerked her head."Yes, *right now*. We need to go. This isn't a joke."

"I need to bring her."

Margie shook her head. "You know that you can't do that."

"Why not? We're married."

"Have you done the paperwork at the embassy?"

"No, but can we do it right now?"

"The American embassy's locked down. And you know that that girl doesn't have a passport, Sam."

"But—"

"Get your stuff. We have to go."

Sam walked into the house holding Pama's hand. Inside he let go of her. He knew that he'd get through it, but what about his perfect native girl? There were other girls, but not where they were taking him—to the U.S.

Mama Dinga rushed inside. "What's happening?" Tata Mukali and Bulu followed.

"I need to go with my boss."

Pama clutched Sam's arm. "Are you taking me to America?"

Sam adjusted his glasses. "I can't, Pama, but—"

"What?" Mama Dinga said.

"You're not taking her to America?" Tata Mukali said.

Pama looked at her father. He moved closer to her.

Sam didn't look at any of them. He went to his dresser. "Don't worry. I'll be back."

Mama Dinga put her hands on her hips. "You know she's a marked woman now."

"I know that." Sam dug through a drawer of clothes for his passport. "I'll be back." Sam thought it best not to look at them.

Mama Dinga stretched her neck forward. "Prove it."

"I said that I'll be back." He slid his passport in his back pocket.

"That's not good enough," Mama Dinga said.

"Okay, I'll leave all my things here."

"With the key to your hut? This is also Pama's house now," Mama Dinga said.

"Sure. It's right there." He pointed to it atop the dresser. Margie honked the horn.

Sam squeezed Pama's hand and walked out. She stood and looked after him.

"I wish you weren't leaving, Sam," Bulu said.

"You can have all of my socks, Bulu."

He climbed into the Land Cruiser. The family stood outside Sam's window. They wore long faces, except for Mama Dinga. Hers was a combination of doubt and anger. Sam waved at them once through the glass. Only Bulu waved.

Margie pulled away, first going slow around the huts until she reached the main road. Then she gunned it. Sam peered at the side mirror for one last look but only saw a cloud of dust.

*

He returned to Olivia. Over a meatloaf dinner his first night back, his brother asked, "What happened to that Palm Tree girl you were engaged to?" Sam's father looked at Sam. His mother stared at her food.

Sam looked at the pool of gravy in his mashed potatoes. "Her name is Pama, and I married her."

His brother and mother looked at his father. He moved his food to the side of his mouth. "So you really went ahead and married that *colored?*"

Sam inhaled slowly. "No, I married an African."

"Oh, you married an *African*. What the hell's the difference?"

Sam ran his fork through the mashed potatoes, flooding his plate with gravy.

During the day, Sam worked on pens, shoveled shit, and fed the pigs. At night he couldn't sleep. He lay awake picturing Pama and other beautiful native girls. Twice a week Sam used the wall-mount phone in his parents' kitchen to call Peace Corps headquarters to see if he would be returning to Zaire. No one at the Zaire desk had an answer for him. Seven weeks passed until Joe Quinlin, the Peace Corps Director for Africa, told him that the growing violence in

Zaire had forced Peace Corps to shut down operations there, but he offered Sam service in any other African country if he wanted.

Sam hung up and slid down the wall. He sat on the linoleum, twisting the phone cord. Sam pictured the family waiting for the sound of the approaching Land Cruiser. He saw Pama sitting in his hut or staring out at the road that would lead her husband back to her. He saw the family eating *fufu*, talking about Sam, wondering when he would return. He felt uneasy. She was a marked woman. It wasn't his fault. There's nothing he could do. He pictured fourteen-year-old girls in other African countries—their young bodies and faces. Sexual flutter filled his stomach.

He immersed himself in work, building new hog pens twelve hours a day. His father and brother left him alone. He worked longer days, searching for the answer. Each day Pama slipped further away, and other African girls replaced her—tall Kenyans, narrow-faced Ethiopians, dark black Sudanese. A month later he looked up from repairing a broken fence rail, unclipped his tool belt and dropped his hammer, and headed into the house.

He dialed 1-800-484-8580.

"Peace Corps," a nasal voice said.

"African Director please." Sam looked out the window at a row of hogs chomping food in the feed cages.

"Hello, Joe Quinlin."

"Mr. Quinlin, this is Sam Tootle. I'll accept your offer to serve in another African country. I'm ready to start over."

# THE WEDDING APARTMENT

Adoni and Irini had dated for seven years, ever since they'd been seniors in high school. He wasn't in a hurry to get married. Like most unmarried Greeks, he lived at home. Some didn't like the cultural tradition, but Adoni wasn't one of them. He worked as a ticket salesman at Thessaloniki's bustling train station, just like his father, who had gotten him the job. Most days he returned home on the city bus, passing the concrete apartment buildings and homes that filled the city, not feeling any better or worse than he had when he'd gone to work. His job was just something he did, so he went along with it without much thought. Irini worked as a high school coach. She liked her job but had grown tired of living at home with her mother. When she complained about it to Adoni, he always changed the subject.

One afternoon Adoni and his parents sat in their modest living room watching the local soccer team, PAOK, play a German team. His mother crocheted doilies next to him on the couch. "Adoni, when you marry Irini years from now, I'll build you an apartment onto the side of this house. There's just enough room."

His father turned toward her. "Don't you know there's a game on? Go to the kitchen if you want to talk."

She sighed, crossed her swollen ankles, and looked down at her fingers working the fine thread. Her round cheeks sagged with age. The flesh on her upper arms hung like a goat's udder. Her thick thighs were covered by a skirt. She looked up at Adoni and whispered, "I will build it for you."

"Shhh," his father said.

Adoni smiled. He'd been with Irini so long that he assumed they'd marry someday. He guessed that's what happened, eventually people just got married.

That night Adoni and Irini went to Katerina's—their favorite *taverna*. They took a city bus to Old Town and walked cobblestone streets lined by two-story homes from the Ottoman Empire. Katerina's white sign lit up part of the dark street. They ate *kalamaria* and *souvlaki*, drank retsina wine. After dinner Adoni lit a Marlboro. Irini looked at her glass of retsina and then up at him. "Do you ever think about us getting married?"

His eyes widened. "Why?"

"Well do you?"

He hated to be put on the spot. A waiter picked up their empty plates and drifted away.

Adoni liked the way things were—the two of them going out throughout the week, meeting with friends at bars and nightclubs, going to the Hotel Hercules to have sex. They'd never talked about getting married. He'd thought maybe sometime in the future he'd talk to her about it, but not anytime soon. He wasn't going to tell her that now.

He flicked ashes into a plastic Olympic Airlines ashtray. "I think about it sometimes." He took a drag.

"Do you want to go downtown this week to look at some rings?"

The back of his neck started to heat up. He exhaled a cloud of smoke. "You want to get married *now?*"

"I'm tired of us not being together all the time. Don't you feel the same?"

He couldn't tell her the truth. He sucked on his cigarette. "Sure."

"So we're going to shop for rings?"

"I guess so." He didn't know what was happening. He'd once been in a car accident. His friend was taking him for a ride in his new

BMW. They were on the highway heading into the hills above the city when his friend lost control. Adoni felt like he was back in that car—everything was suddenly spinning so fast, nothing was clear, lines of colors raced by the windshield, and all he could do was hold on and wait for it to stop, hopefully without hitting something.

Irini slid her hand across the paper tablecloth and took hold of Adoni's. All of her smiled—her dark eyes, pear-shaped nose, big lips, white teeth. Adoni smiled with his mouth closed.

They held hands for a few seconds. Then he remembered his goal. Adoni pulled his hand away, grabbed his Marlboros from his leather jacket, and lit one.

"You look worried," she said.

He took a long drag.

"What's wrong, Adoni?"

He couldn't tell her that he didn't want to put money into a wedding. He'd been saving for a motorcycle—a tough-looking dirt bike like the one the guy rode in the Odyssey Cologne commercial. He was tired of taking the bus everywhere, especially to the Hercules.

Once a week they visited the Hotel Hercules. Its cement walls blackened from pollution, the Hercules was one of the only hotels in Thessaloniki that rented rooms by the hour. They first went there on the night of their high school graduation. It was Irini's idea. At first Adoni was scared to do something his mother wouldn't approve of, but Irini insisted. She knew what to do, and Adoni liked it. He still did. Afterward they'd wait at a nearby bus stop for the last 152. One high-heeled foot on the curb, the other in the street, Irini would watch for the bus while Adoni stayed on the sidewalk. He'd check out Irini's short, stylish hair and tall, muscled body. He felt proud to be the boyfriend of a star athlete. He hated that they took the bus after visiting the Hercules. It felt trashy. He had to get that motorcycle.

Irini looked at him from across the table and said, "What's wrong?"

"Are you sure we're ready?"

"I am, aren't you?"

"Sure." So they were engaged. He'd always thought getting engaged meant surprising his bride with a ring while watching a sunset, like in the movies. He didn't know what to think now. He just wished that he could talk with his mother about it, and just let it all sit for a year or two. But when Irini wanted something, she had to have it right then. He knew her too well. This whole thing was already spinning out of control. He couldn't stop it, just as he couldn't stop his friend's BMW from slamming into the highway divider.

"Good. Does your family have money for the wedding?"

"I'll ask them." He couldn't mention his motorcycle money or that his cheap father probably wouldn't give a euro. He wasn't sure how he was going to tell his mother.

"Maybe there's some extra money in my wedding fund. I'll ask my mother," Irini said. After her father died of a stroke, her mother had told her that they'd set aside money for a small wedding reception.

"Okay, but I'll buy your ring." He couldn't let her family pay for *that*.

*

The next morning Irini and her mother sat at the small wooden table in their sunlit kitchen. Grape leaves sprang from vines outside the window. Irini sliced fresh bread, sweetened her mother's Turkish coffee to her liking, and placed her breakfast on the table next to the framed picture of her mustached father. Her mother did her cross and bit into some bread. "Bravo, Irini, it's still warm." Irini smiled and sipped her coffee.

"Adoni and I are going to look for my ring, *mamá*."

Her mother raised her eyebrows. "Did that boy ask you to marry him?"

"We talked about it last night."

"Did he drop to his knee?"

"No, we talked about it after dinner."

Her mother raised her eyebrows. "What, men today don't ask women to marry them the right way?"

"We're past that, *mamá*."

"Oh, you're *past that*. And I guess he's past asking me for your hand?"

"Oh, *mamá*."

"Don't 'Oh, *mamá*,' me. You're father would not approve, and you know it. You were on Greece's Olympic Volleyball team. You deserve a champion, not a mama's boy."

Irini had been the team's greatest weapon. Her vicious spike led Greece into the quarterfinals at the Athens 2004 Games. A Greek weightlifter, an Italian rower, and a Brazilian discus thrower had pursued her, but they were boisterous athletic types. She loved her Adoni, who sat behind the team bench at all her games.

Irini sipped her coffee. "You've known that we were going to get married."

"I know, but what's right is what's right."

Her mother took the picture of her husband and ran it over her black skirt to rid it of dust.

"*Mamá*," Irini started.

Her mother looked up.

"Adoni needs help with some expenses."

Her mother raised her eyebrows. "Oh?"

"We need money for his suit, the church, and the priest."

"Does he need us to buy his socks and underwear too?"

"*Mamá!*"

"*Ella*, Irini. That boy has a job. Where's his money going?"

"He's saving for our home."

"Your home?—Ha! His mother will give you her bedroom before she lets her son leave that house, and you know it."

Both families had attended St. Elias church, and the children had gone to the same schools, but the adults had never been close. Irini's parents thought the other family was lazy. Adoni's mother thought those people were too aggressive. His father dismissed them because Irini's father hadn't been a PAOK fan.

"Anyway, is there an extra 1,200 euros in my wedding fund?"

"Irini, your father was a welder, not an Onassis. His pension doesn't give us much."

Irini stirred her coffee. "Hey, maybe Uncle Dino can help us."

"If you want money from my brother, you call him. But be careful."

"I know what to say to him."

"Oh yeah?"

Irini grabbed the phone from the tile counter and dialed her uncle's main real estate office. She owed him a lot. When she was twelve, he had seen her play volleyball and recognized a champion. He told her mother and father how to grow an Olympian. He knew all about it— he was the 1967 European Greco-Roman wrestling champion in the middle-weight division. He was expected to medal at the 1968 Olympics in Mexico City, but an Achilles tendon injury took him out in the first round. Still, his star status was solidified in Greece, and his real estate business skyrocketed. Billboards around Thessaloniki showed his pitted face and winning smile above his motto, "I wrestle the best deal for you."

"*Yiasou*, Uncle Dino. It's Irini."

"*Yiasou, pedi mou*—my child. What a nice surprise. What's new?"

"A lot—Adoni and I are engaged."

"Congratulations! You'll be the perfect bride. That Adoni is a lucky man. If he doesn't treat you right, I'll twist him into a German pretzel."

"I know you will, Uncle Dino. I wanted to ask you something: Can you give me away?"

Her mother shook her head and did her cross. "My God, you're buying him with affection," she whispered.

"You really want me to give you away?"

"Yes, yes, Uncle Dino."

His voice cracked, "Oh, *pedi mou*, I'd be honored."

Irini put her hand over the receiver. "He's crying."

"Shame on you."

He sniffled. "Is there anything you need?"

"Actually, we're short a little money for some unexpected expenses."

"Maybe I can drop off a check this weekend."

"Make it for 1,200 euros."

"Okay, 1,200 euros. Listen, a client just arrived, so I have to go. Give your mother a kiss for me. *Yiasou.*"

"*Yiasou.*" She hung up, and smiled at her mother.

"Your father is turning over in his grave."

Three blocks away at Adoni's family's home, his father read the PAOK soccer stats and chomped on a *bougatza*, littering his mustache with flakes of filo and dollops of custard. His mother shuffled about the kitchen in her cheap slippers. She spread marmalade on Adoni's toast and made his coffee while Adoni sat at the white Formica table thinking about the best way to tell her. He hadn't seen his parents laugh together for years. All he saw was his mother cook, clean, and stay out of the way of his father's PAOK addiction. Adoni listened to his mother's stories about growing up in a village, often accompanied her to the outdoor market, and sometimes took her shopping for a new dress or skirt. The thought of his mother feeling more alone and unappreciated once he married Irini tore at his stomach. But he was meeting Irini that afternoon for coffee, and she would want to know if they offered wedding money. His mother set the toast and coffee in front of him, fetched Adoni's blue uniform, and set up an ironing board. He stared out the window at their neighbors' square concrete home that looked like theirs. When his mother finished ironing his uniform, she hung it in his closet and wheeled her wire shopping basket from the back porch.

"You look pale, *pedi mou*," she said. "Are you sick?" She felt his forehead.

"Irini and I are engaged."

Her eyes widened. "What did you say?"

His father didn't look up from his paper.

"Irini and I are engaged." He looked down at the table and shook a Marlboro from his pack.

Her eyes began to water. "Did you hear that, Theo? He's engaged."

"Huh?"

"Adoni said he and Irini are engaged."

The father reached across the table and shook Adoni's hand. "Congratulations, son."

Adoni nodded. Maybe his father would smooth it out. At work when a customer complained about ticket prices or demanded a refund because they missed a train, he always had his father handle it.

"Is that all you're going to say?" his mother said. She grabbed a tissue and wiped her eyes. "You're not going to question his decision, Theo? They're very young."

"The boy's twenty five, Cleo. Weren't we twenty?"

"Things were different back then. Irini's very demanding, you know."

"If Adoni loves Irini, he'll figure out how to handle her, like I did you." He winked.

Adoni smiled.

"Theo, if I controlled you, you would be married to me, not PAOK."

"Leave my PAOK out of it. A man has to have some pleasure in life."

"They're just so young." She went to the sink to wash the dishes, handling each one slowly as she stared out the window. "At least they'll live here."

"Where, in the closet?" Adoni's father asked.

"I'm going to build an apartment on the side of the house, like I told you."

"You still have that dumb idea in your head? That's a bad way to spend your inheritance money."

"It's my money from my dead father." She did her cross. "I'd rather build them an apartment next to our home than spend it on a wedding. They'll have their apartment for years, until we die, then they'll live in this house."

Adoni pictured him and Irini living in an apartment next door and someday in the family home. It felt right.

"We should use some of that money on the wedding, Cleo. We can't let Irini's mother pay for everything."

"I'm not asking her to help pay for the apartment, so she shouldn't expect money for the wedding."

"That's not right."

"Then you sell your season tickets and give them some money for the wedding."

"Leave my PAOK out of this."

"Adoni likes the apartment idea, don't you, Adoni?"

"Yes, *mamá*." He wondered how he'd sell the idea to Irini.

"See," she said and grabbed her shopping basket.

"It's your money," Adonis' father said, dropping his head into his paper. Adoni's mother waddled out the door pulling her basket behind her. Adoni watched his cigarette burn in the ashtray. Being there for his mother and living with Irini under the same roof was the perfect scenario, but he wasn't sure Irini would go for it. He took a drag from his cigarette. His mother's basket rattled down the sidewalk.

*

Adoni and Irini met at a neighborhood café and sat outside in the spring sun. Irini wore her blue and white Olympic sweats, Adoni his jeans and cowboy boots, like the man on the Marlboro billboards. Other young couples sat at tables drinking frappé, Nescafe, and orange juice. Cars, scooters, and city buses ambled through the round-about in front of the café.

Irini smiled. "I got the money for your suit, the church, and the priest."

"Really? How'd you do that?"

"I asked my Uncle Dino to give me away."

Adoni smiled. "You're incredible." Maybe the motorcycle was still possible, he thought.

"What did your parents offer to pay for?"

"Our apartment."

Irini's eyebrows shot up. "They're going to help us rent an apartment?"

"Not exactly." He couldn't look at her. Two teenage boys on a scooter zipped around an Alpha Romeo in the round-about. Adoni shifted in his seat. "My mother is going to build us an apartment alongside our house."

"What?"

"It'll be great. You won't have to cook or wash my uniform."

Her eyes locked onto his. "I'm not marrying you to live with your parents, Adoni."

It felt like pliers were twisting his stomach. He wanted someone else to deal with it, but he also wanted to live with Irini in the apartment. "How can I tell my mother not to build it? It's a huge gift."

"It's a gift for herself, and you know it."

He didn't like how direct she could be. "Don't talk about my mother like that."

"So you *like* the idea?"

"Think about it: we'll be able to save a lot of money. Then we can buy our own place." He didn't like to lie, but he couldn't tell her about the plan to move into his family home. "If we refuse her gift, we'll hurt her. And I can't do that."

"Why not?"

"Because I can't let her down."

Irini leaned forward. "But it's okay to hurt me? That's bullshit, Adoni. You just want her to keep spoiling you." Her voice rose. "What about me? I'm going to be your wife."

A couple at another table glanced at them. He hated her angry side. The pliers pinching his stomach twisted again.

"Please, settle down."

"Why should I when you don't have the balls to do what's right?"

Adoni turned away. She didn't understand his mother's situation, and she didn't understand duty. A yellow Yugo stalled in the round-about.

"My mother doesn't have anyone but me."

"You can still be there for her without living with her."

He knew she was right, but he couldn't move out. He couldn't hurt his mother. And Irini wouldn't do everything for him like his mother.

"I can't turn down her gift."

"That doesn't mean we'll live there."

Cars honked at the Yugo. The man behind the wheel tried to start it, but it wouldn't turn over. A bus started honking.

"Let's go help them," Irini said.

"They'll figure it out."

"My God, Adoni, do something for once."

He looked at her blankly.

Irini and a man from another table ran toward the car. The driver got out of the Yugo and began to push from the door frame. Irini and the man pushed from the rear. They rolled it out of the round-about. Adoni watched.

*

At Uncle Dino's big house in Panorama, the two families gathered for an engagement party on his massive veranda. All of Thessaloniki lay below, hugging the wide bay of water that was more gray than blue. Uncle Dino poured ouzo and retsina and encouraged his guests to enjoy the spread of lamb, *dolmathes*, *spanikopita*, *mousaka*, and different salads.

The mothers greeted each other and exchanged small talk. Irini's great aunt, uncle, and cousins from Athens joked about Uncle Dino's habit of having too much to eat, as he did every Easter when he hosted the family for a food marathon. Adoni's father stood aside drinking glasses of ouzo. Irini hooked her arm through Adoni's and didn't let go. That morning on the phone Adoni had laid out his argument for moving into the apartment—they'd save money, not have to cook, he'd be close to his mother. Irini said, "No, no, no." In his mind she didn't have a choice. She'll give in, he thought. She was aggressive, but he was going to be her husband. Just because a woman objected to something didn't mean anything in the end.

Adoni's cousin asked him where they were going to live.

"With us, in the apartment we're building," Adoni's mother said. "Builders are working on it day and night to have it ready before the wedding."

Irini's mother raised her eyebrows and looked at Irini, who looked at her mother and shook her head just enough.

After more ouzo, Adoni's father picked up a conversation with Uncle Dino, also a PAOK fanatic. Adoni's father nearly slurred his words. They talked about PAOK's 1983 championship game against rival Aris. They lamented the death of Stamidis, the great PAOK forward who crashed his Maserati into a tree. Uncle Dino led Adoni's father to the dining room. A framed white and black PAOK jersey with Stamidis's autograph below the PAOK shield hung on the wall. Adoni's father steadied himself with a chair and moved from within a centimeter of it. "It's beautiful. How did you get it?" he said, accidentally spitting on the glass.

Uncle Dino wiped the glass with his handkerchief. "I helped Stamidis buy his first home—a Spanish style mansion with a full bar, pool, and sauna. He was a good guy."

They turned to look at the view through the window. Adoni's father held on to the back of the chair. The deep orange sun hung over the bay. The guests were laughing at something Irini's great aunt had said.

"Thank you for hosting us."

"My pleasure. It feels good to have the families together. Their wedding will be wonderful. So I hear you're building the kids an apartment."

"Huh? Oh, my wife is. I don't like the idea, but she needs her son to be close to her." He paused. "Listen, I know you've already paid the priest and all, but we're PAOK brothers. I want us to help pay." He sipped from his ouzo. "We'll pay for half of the reception."

"Are you sure?"

"Yes, I'm serious. I told her that she should use some of her inheritance money on the wedding."

"I know my sister would appreciate it. Things have been really tight for her." Uncle Dino poured Adoni's father more ouzo.

"It's a deal," Adoni's father said, glassy eyed. They clinked glasses.

\*

Irini made the morning coffee and splayed the classifieds of the *Thessaloniki Liberty* on the kitchen table. Her mother came in wearing her nightgown. "What are you looking for, *pedi mou?*"

"An apartment."

"Bravo. Does Adoni's mother know?"

Irini skimmed the paper. "No, and neither does Adoni."

"You're smart."

Irini found some affordable one-bedrooms in their area, but they were too close to his mother. Then she saw one in Old Town: "Small, one bedroom apartment. Available July 1. Call 238.362." Irini dialed the number and looked at the picture of her father on the table. He would have been proud of her. He had taught Irini to strike before being struck. When she had played volleyball, she used to identify the best player on the opposing team. Early in the game, she'd spike one into her chest or stomach to beat on her confidence. It usually worked.

"Why are you calling someone at 7:30?" her mother asked.

"I have to, *mamá.*"

She took a bus to Old Town and found the apartment. The gray building with peeling green trim was a block from Katerina's. Single hanging light bulbs hardly lit the stairway. Scratched walls led to the small unheated apartment. The bathroom was so tiny that its door opened half way before hitting the toilet. The thin carpet in the triangular bedroom was nearly worn through. A metal table and two folding chairs sat in the kitchen, a stiff old couch and rattan chair in the front room, and a lumpy twin bed in the bedroom. Irini signed the lease and handed the landlord a wad of euros.

Every day for a week Irini went to the apartment after work. She scrubbed the walls, bleached the bathroom, washed the carpet. She hung white curtains in the kitchen and photographs of Olympia in the front room. A few weeks later, just before the wedding, she stocked the cupboard with olive oil, rice, lentils, and the fridge with feta and olives.

*

The builders put the finishing touches on the apartment. Adoni's mother wanted to paint the interior white, but Adoni insisted that they paint their bedroom Irini's favorite color—blue. He framed and hung some photos of them in the small living room. He built a flower box outside the kitchen window and planted her favorite flowers—tulips. He was excited. He pictured waking up next to Irini and then going next door to have breakfast with his mother. And coming home from work to his mother rolling *dolmathes* or stuffing cabbage or grilling octopus. They'd all eat together in the main house and then watch TV in the living room. When the PAOK games were on, he and his mother could go talk in the apartment. He and Irini would have their alone time in the apartment. They wouldn't have to go to the Hercules ever again. It would all be so easy. Irini would change her mind once she saw the apartment and realized how easy it would be for her. Adoni and his mother walked through the apartment one more time. He turned toward her and said, "Thank you, *mamá*," kissing her on the cheek. Her eyes watered as she smiled.

*

The small Byzantine church in their neighborhood glowed in early evening light when the fifty friends and family members followed Irini and Adoni outside. Irini's bronze body made her white dress with its thick shoulder straps look whiter. Her satin high-heels made her even taller than Adoni, who looked small in his dark blue suit. His mother had made him buy the next size up, saying that every married man gains weight. Uncle Dino arranged to have a line of blue and white taxis outside of the church for the couple, families, and guests.

Three days before their wedding, Adoni had bought his dirt bike. He surprised Irini that night and proudly took her to the Hercules. When she asked where he got the money, he didn't answer. He wanted them to ride it to the reception, but Irini refused. Outside the church, Uncle Dino opened the door of the first cab for Irini and Adoni. Their cab led the way to Katerina's.

Irini hooked her arm around Adoni's neck and pulled him to her.

The cab stopped at a stoplight next to a Roman arch. Three scooters pulled in front of the cab.

"I have a surprise for you," Irini said. Her eyes smiled.

Adoni looked at her.

"I got us our own apartment."

"What do you mean?"

"I rented us an apartment a block from Katerina's. We'll pass by it soon. Tonight we'll be able to walk to our own home."

"What are you saying? Why did you keep this a secret?"

"Just like your secret motorcycle money." She raised her eyebrows and looked at him without blinking.

He turned toward the window. He pictured the beautiful apartment his mother had built and filled with new everything. Anger tore open his stomach. His mother had spent all of her inheritance. She didn't even have money for a new dress or shoes for the wedding.

"But my mother built us a beautiful apartment."

Irini looked out her window. "I told you I didn't want to live there."

"She spent all of her money and customized it to suit you!"

"That's nice, but I won't live with your parents," she said, still looking out her window.

"What about the sacrifice my mother made for us?"

"It's not my fault. You should have told her that I didn't want it."

"I'm your husband now, Irini."

She turned and looked at him. "That's right, so I come first."

Adoni looked out the window at dirty concrete buildings and

people walking along the sidewalk. He pulled a cigarette from his inside pocket and leaned toward the cab driver. "Do you mind if I smoke?"

"It's your wedding day, do whatever you want."

Adoni lit up.

"Slow down please," Irini said to the driver. "Here it is." She pointed at the apartment building. "Do you like it?"

"My God, it's older than the Acropolis. You chose *this* over a new apartment?"

Irini didn't say anything. Smoke drifted between them. Adoni took another drag. He pictured his mother crying as she locked the door to the apartment, never to re-enter it, the pain of it growing each time she saw it protruding from the side of her house like a tumor.

*

Irini and Adoni greeted their guests outside Katerina's, kissing everyone on both cheeks. They didn't look at each other, but they laughed together when Irini's great aunt said, "You need to make a baby, *tonight*."

A three piece band of bouzouki, clarinet, and drums set up in the corner. The immediate families sat opposite each other at one table with Irini and Adoni in the middle. Irini told everyone about her great aunt's comment, and they all laughed. Uncle Dino raised his glass. "To their hundred children." The mothers talked about becoming *yia yias*.

"Won't it be wonderful to take our grandchildren to the park, Cleo?" Irini's mother said.

"Yes, yes, Stella. It will be wonderful to have a baby at our home. You'll have to visit whenever you want."

Waiters covered the tables with bowls of feta and olives, plates of bread, and platters of lamb, *spanikopita*, *mousaka*, and *pastitzo*.

"Hey, Theo," Uncle Dino said, "we'll dress their son in a PAOK uniform."

"Now we're talking about something important," Adoni's father said.

"And if they have a girl?" Irini's mother said.

"Yeah, if they have a girl?" Adoni's mother said, raising her glass to Irini's mother.

"Then she'll wear the PAOK uniform!" Uncle Dino said.

They all laughed. The mothers rolled their eyes and smiled.

Everyone cut into their thick slices of lamb, chipped away at mounds of *moussaka*, spread *tarama* on chunks of bread.

"Excellent food, eh Dino?" Adoni's father said.

"You can't go wrong at Katerina's. Oh, thanks again for your generous offer."

Adoni's father looked at Uncle Dino for an explanation, but Uncle Dino turned to talk to the waiter about bringing out more of everything.

Adoni's mother leaned toward her husband's ear and asked, "What offer?"

"I don't know."

They returned to their food.

Guests moved tables aside as the band started to play the Zorba song. Irini stood up, kicked off her high heels, and led Adoni to dance.

"Bravo *pedia*," guests shouted.

She jumped and kicked and slapped her heels like an acrobat.

"*Yiasou* Irini!" guests shouted.

The band played other songs, and Uncle Dino, Irini's mother, and some guests joined Irini and Adoni.

The waiters removed empty plates from the table and replaced them with platters of *baklava* and pots of coffee. The owner turned on the light outside. It flickered a few times before lighting up the front of Katerina's.

Uncle Dino and Irini's mother returned to the table. They ate *baklava* and sipped coffee with Adoni's parents. Irini and Adoni danced in a circle with the others, as the small band played long folk songs.

Irini's great aunt and other elderly guests kissed Irini and Adoni goodbye and shuffled out the door into the dark night. A waiter set an adding machine on the counter in front of the kitchen and started punching in figures.

The waiter approached Adoni's mother with the bill. "That goes to her," she said, motioning to Irini's mother, who raised her eyebrows. The waiter handed Irini's mother the bill. She took it and placed it between herself and Adoni's mother, and said, "How should we handle paying our shares?"

"What shares?"

"You agreed to pay half."

"I'm sorry, but we never agreed to that."

Irini's mother looked at Uncle Dino, who looked at Theo. "Remember at my home when you offered to pay for half of the reception?"

"I did?"

"Yeah, after looking at Stamidis's jersey."

"Oh yeah, Stamidis's jersey. It's in a frame, right?"

Adoni and Irini walked up holding hands and smiling.

"Yes. I'd told you about selling him his home. We were checking out the view when you offered to pay half."

"What are you talking about?" Irini asked.

Nobody answered her.

Adoni's father looked at Uncle Dino. "I don't remember anything like that."

"You were drinking a lot of ouzo that afternoon."

Adoni's father turned red.

"Did you offer to pay half of the bill?" Adoni's mother asked him.

"Honestly, I can't remember."

She bit her top lip and twisted a cloth napkin with her fingers. "You must have because Dino wouldn't make it up. How could you do that? You knew we didn't have any extra money. We built the kids an apartment."

The band stopped playing. The guests clapped and started toward their tables.

Adoni's father stared at her without blinking. "I really don't remember."

Adoni couldn't look at his father or at Uncle Dino and Irini's mother. He'd seen his father drink too much at parties before and forget what happened. He was embarrassed, but he knew Irini's rich uncle would take care of it. He was concerned about his mother. Her face had turned white.

Some guests walked toward them but turned and walked outside when they noticed the families talking among themselves.

"I've never been so ashamed in my life, Theo," Adoni's mother said. She turned to Irini's mother. "I'm so sorry, but we don't have the money to help with this. All we can offer is the apartment."

"That's not right," Uncle Dino said. "He offered."

"I'm sorry, I'm sorry, but we don't have any money left," Adoni's mother said in a pleading voice.

Irini's mother turned toward Uncle Dino. "Let it go. She doesn't have the money because of the apartment."

"But we're not going to live there," Irini said.

Adoni's mother jerked her head toward Irini. "Huh?"

"I rented us an apartment a block from here. We're going to live there."

"Please, Irini, not now," Adoni said.

"Why not?"

"Please."

His mother looked at him. "Is this true, Adoni?"

"Tell her," Irini said to Adoni. "She needs to know the truth."

Adoni's mother looked like Irini had slapped her twice. Her eyes moved from Irini to Adoni. "You're not going to live in the apartment? I paid extra for the builder to finish it in time. We made it perfect for you, just like you would want it. And now you *don't* want it? You *don't* want it?" Her eyes blinked and her chin quivered.

"*Ella, mamá.* Let's go outside," Adoni said. He led her out. His father followed.

The guests had lined up alongside the *tavern* and were talking. They went silent when Adoni and his mother and then his father emerged. They walked down the cobblestone street a few meters until his mother stopped.

"How could you do this to me, Adoni?" his mother said. Tears streamed down her cheeks. "My father worked hard all his life as a plumber, and I used everything he left me to build you and Irini an apartment that you don't want. Why didn't you tell me?"

"I want to live there, *mamá.* Irini rented the other apartment on her own. She just told me on the way to the reception."

"Well you don't have to live there. You can live in ours."

She started walking slowly. Adoni walked beside her. His father followed them. Irini knew that renting an apartment would hurt his mother, but she still did it. And behind his back. He pictured her going to that dump and doing it all without him. He wasn't surprised, but that didn't mean that he had to live there.

"Let's go home," Adoni said.

"Are you going to get Irini?" his father asked.

"I'll talk to her later."

Adoni wrapped his arm around his mother's shoulder. She needed him. He'd call Irini later and tell her that they would live in the new apartment. They started down the cobblestone street. His father followed.

Irini bolted out the door past the silent guests and into the street, her high heels sounding like a thoroughbred. She stopped and stood in the light of Katerina's sign and looked down the street at them. They were far enough away that they were nearly out of the light. Irini placed one hand on her hip and leaned forward, her neck jutting out. "Adoni, if you go home with her, you stay there!"

Adoni stopped and turned around. He looked at Irini, who stared at him, still leaning forward like the statue of Nike.

"Please, Adoni," his mother said and grabbed his arm. "Let's go home."

He looked at Irini. She stood still. Katerina's fluorescent sign hummed. He knew that she meant it. She'd go to the church the next day to annul their marriage, send him her ring, and march right into another man's life.

Adoni pulled his arm from his mother.

"Adoni?" his mother said.

He started walking toward Irini, taking small steps.

"Adoni?" his mother said.

He kept walking toward Irini, taking small steps.

"Adoni, *ella, pedi mou*," his mother said. Her eyes reaching out for him. "Adoni, let's go home."

He kept walking toward Irini. He knew that if he looked back then, he'd go to his mother.

Adoni reached Irini. She wrapped her arm around his waist, swung him around in the opposite direction, and they started toward their rented apartment, Irini's heels steadily striking the old street. Adoni looked back. His mother stood there, staring, pleading. He felt Irini's hand on him leading him away. There was nothing that he could do now. It was out of his control. There was nothing he could do.

# WEIGHING THE OPTIONS

Lately Sharon had been thinking about her roots—growing up in the middle of an almond orchard outside Merced, in California's flat Central Valley. Random images of her past were brought on by the San Francisco hills she walked and drove, by the cold, foggy days in July, and by the sounds of city busses, car alarms, and sirens. She saw images of playing in the orchard and going to a small country school with kids just like her, who wore jeans and shot gophers with BB guns and rode in the backs of their fathers' Chevy or Ford trucks. She saw the rows of almond trees that surrounded their house and filled the 400-acre orchard her father managed, she and her sister riding bikes through them, climbing them, necking with country boys under them. She saw the cord of almond wood she and her father loaded and delivered to someone in the mountains and felt the shame that ignited her determination to break out of that life.

She and her father had delivered the wood to his boss's friend up near Yosemite. The friend managed the Tenaya Lodge. As a perk, the boss said that they could take a swim in the Lodge's pool.

After unloading the wood, they drove their dusty truck to the big hotel made of granite and redwood, the kind of place she'd only seen on TV. They went around back and parked. In the truck, she changed into her one piece, a hand-me-down from her sister. Her father changed behind a dumpster at the end of the parking lot. His thin, white torso stood out against his red neck and muscled arms. He grabbed two towels. Feeling nervous, she followed him to a backdoor. A sign read, "Pool 1ˢᵗ Floor." Maroon carpet with yellow squares running down the middle led to an elevator with gold metal doors. She stared at her and her father's reflections, focusing on their dusty faces and white bodies and dirty fingernails.

Just then a family of three walked up, all wearing white robes that said Tenaya Lodge and holding fluffy white towels. The mother and father didn't look at them, but the daughter, who also looked twelve, stared at them, at his frayed swim trunks and then at her cheap bathing suit, her old towel, the scabs on her knees, the dirt under her fingernails, her tomboy haircut.

When the elevator doors opened, Sharon hoped that her father would let them take it, but he walked in first, his back white as a patch of snow. She followed, and the family followed her. As the elevator descended, she glanced at the girl. Her finger *and* toenails were painted red. Her wispy blond hair was up in a bun. She wore mascara. It didn't look like she'd been dirty a day in her life.

The elevator doors opened, and a big indoor pool spread out sideways in front of them. Everything sparkled and looked rich. Some kids volleyed a beach ball in the pool. A hot tub sat in the corner. The girl slipped off her robe. Her two-piece bathing suit had bows on the hips and shoulders. She eased into the hot tub like she'd done it a thousand times before.

"How about sitting in the hot tub?" Sharon's father asked.

She didn't want to be near the girl, but she didn't want to say no to her father.

"Okay, dad."

They went in. The girl didn't look at her at all. But Sharon snuck glances at her. She was perfect.

During the drive home, the girl was heavy on Sharon's mind. The more she thought of her, the more worthless she felt. It was horrible, feeling those feelings.

It was easy to call up that time, but that was 25 years ago. Now she had a family, lived in a fabulous house, didn't have to work, devoted most of her time to Lily. It's not that she was unhappy, it's just that something wasn't right. She felt like a boat whose anchor had unknowingly been pulled up, allowing it to drift away from something essential.

All this ran through her mind as she brushed her short hair and looked in the mirror. Bags hung under her eyes. She could never sleep when Lars was away. She looked out the window. Ugh, more San Francisco fog.

"Mom," Lily called from her room, "Muffin's still making that sound."

"Okay, I'll check on him in a second. Are you getting dressed, sweetie? We have to leave in fifteen minutes."

"I'm not going to school, mommy—Muffin's sick."

"Please get dressed, sweetie."

"No! I'm not going to school," she whined.

"Please, sweetie, let's not do this."

"School's stupid!"

The week before, Sharon had let Lily stay home from school two days because she didn't want to go. She had to convince her to go.

"If you go to school, we can get gelato later."

"Only if I can get gelato tomorrow too. Double chocolate fudge."

"You got a deal, gelato today and tomorrow." Sharon felt a great sense of relief.

"But Muffin's sick. You have to take him to Dr. White."

Sharon put on a black velour sweat suit and went to Lily's room.

"Honey, we have to leave soon. Please get out of your pajamas and into your clothes."

"I need help."

"Sweetie, you're eight years old."

"I need help, mommy," Lily whined.

Sharon pulled Lily's pajama top and bottoms off her and took out a corduroy dress from her closet.

"I hate that dress."

"But it's so cute."

"No it's not. It's stupid. I want the red one with flowers."

Sharon pulled the flower dress off a hanger and put it on Lily, and then she knelt next to the triple-level hamster cage in Lily's room. Muffin lay on his belly and just stared out. He was a typical brown and white hamster, but his head was completely brown. His torso was covered by a blue fleece sweater they'd put on him the night before. Sharon put her ear to the cage. Lily was right, Muffin was wheezing. She picked Lily's pajamas off the floor and folded them, thinking. After dropping off Lily she'd take Muffin to the vet as Lily wanted.

At Lily's school, right before getting out, Lily said, "Mommy, is Muffin going to die?"

Sharon looked into the rear view mirror. Lily was staring at her.

"No, baby, Muffin's just a little sick. Dr. White will give him some medicine, and he'll be fine."

"You promise, mommy."

"I promise, sweetie."

Sharon watched Lily walk into the art deco building and then looked at Muffin in his cage on the passenger's seat. She couldn't believe she was taking a hamster to the vet.

\*

Dr. White's office got Muffin in right away. When the vet tech heard Muffin's wheez, she said, "I need to get the doctor," and hurried out of the examination room.

Maybe Muffin was sicker than she had thought.

The tech returned with Dr. White, who gave Sharon a friendly nod and placed the end of his stethoscope on Muffin's back. He listened and then moved it to a different spot.

Dr. White looked at the tech. "We'll need oxygen." The tech left the room. Sharon looked at Dr. White, confused. He jotted a note onto his clipboard and looked at her. "Poor Muffin's lungs have fluid in them, and his heart is beating too fast. We're going to get him started on some O2. That'll give him a boost. In the meantime, I'd like to run a full blood panel. How's this sound to you?"

Oxygen and blood work for a hamster? It seemed ridiculous, but of course she agreed to it—Muffin was Lily's pet.

"Dr. White," she said, "is Muffin going to be all right?"

"We'll see. His little body is fighting something big."

"How big?"

"It could be fatal, but we're going to do everything we can to make sure that doesn't happen."

Fatal? She pictured Lily running up to their car smiling, excited to get home to see Muffin. How would she face Lily if this didn't happen? Why had she promised her that Muffin would be fine? What would she tell Lily?

The vet tech returned and placed a conical oxygen mask around Muffin's snout and switched on the machine. It made a fast pumping sound. Muffin didn't move.

Sharon had no idea that hamsters received such treatments. When she was growing up, only their hunting dogs went to the vet. They had cats that they underfed so that they wouldn't lose their appetite for mice, rats, and gophers. They never took them to the vet. Their cats sometimes got sick and maybe died from illnesses a vet could have cured or prevented, but her parents didn't make anything of it, and life went on. But that was in Merced.

Sharon watched Muffin and thought about her first step to escape her life in Merced. After the incident at the Tenaya Lodge, she started babysitting. To get rich, she'd need to go to college, and college took money. She earned three dollars on her first job. When she got home that evening, she ironed the bills and placed them in an envelope she kept under her bed. The envelope got fatter every week. By high school, she had stacks of filled envelopes.

She remembered watching the rich kids at Merced High. They were like the girl at the Tenaya Lodge: they had this confidence about them, as if they knew how to walk through a fancy hotel and slip into a hot tub like it was no big deal. They wore sweatshirts that said CAL, UCLA, Boston College, Stanford. Seeing them made Sharon feel ignorant. She wanted to prove herself. She started to study hard. She was in the advanced track with mainly rich kids. They didn't notice her, a Wrangler-jeans, t-shirt-wearing, plain-faced girl who sat in the back. Each year that passed the more she heard about different colleges: UC Santa Barbara, UC Davis, Cal Poly, and the fallback—Stan State. But when someone referred to Berkeley or Stanford, she noticed an admiration and respect that the other schools didn't command. She made a deal with herself to go to one of those someday.

After school, on weekends, and during school breaks, she worked with her father in the almonds. She helped him irrigate in 100-degree heat, harvest in clouds of dust, and prune in bone-chilling cold. And she studied. She earned straight A's. In the spring of her senior year, every week she'd hear someone in class say they were going to Fresno State, another to Davis, another to UOP, and so on. She was jealous that they were going away to college because their families had the money, but nobody in her class got into Cal or Stanford. She knew she'd be going to the local community college—the butt of many jokes. Even her calculus teacher once said to a boy in her class, "If you don't get your act together, you'll be at Merced College next year."

She felt like a flunky by going to Merced College but those feelings burned off when she saw that it would lead her to Berkeley or Stanford without putting a dent in her stash. She took to psychology and made it her major. One day in the college library she spotted the college ranking edition of *US News and World Report*. Stanford was number one in the nation. She studied harder. She applied for Rotary, Lions, and Kiwanis scholarships and got them. Berkeley and Stanford accepted her. Stanford offered her a merit scholarship and she went. She'd broken free.

*

Dr. White asked Sharon to wait in the waiting room. She sat down on a green leather couch next to a wall fountain. A woman with a white bunny was on the other couch next to another woman with a chinchilla.

Someone's cell phone rang. The woman with the chinchilla pulled her phone from her bag. "Hi. I know I'm late. I'm still at the vet's. They're taking *for-ever*. I don't know, I'll check." The woman hung up and approached the receptionist's counter. "Can you tell me why it's taking so long? When I called, you said you'd get us right in."

Sharon was still taken aback by bossy rich people, even though she'd lived in the Bay Area seventeen years. Sure, Stanford had rich kids, but it also had a lot of people who didn't come from money. It wasn't until she got on in Google's HR department that she started to live the Bay Area lifestyle. She'd never known people who got weekly massages, paid $50 for a t-shirt, ate sushi daily. Suddenly she was able to live the side of life she'd first seen at the Tenaya Lodge. She discovered Patron margaritas, Lucky Jeans, wind surfing, and wine tasting. She could afford them, and she wanted them.

She would remember going home to Merced and noticing how simple her family was. Just farm work, Wranglers and white t-shirts, meat and potatoes, and bad TV—the result of no education, she thought. Her father complained a lot about the owner being cheap, but it wasn't like he'd ever leave his job. What else could he do? Her sister had married a dairy farmer, so her life wasn't any better.

Sharon knew that her job gave her a new life, but Lars took her to the next level. He was a programmer at Google. He'd grown up in Chicago and had graduated from Stanford two years before Sharon got there. He was so worldly. He knew about cultural things—art, literature, theater, food, wine—and he'd traveled around the globe. What he saw in her, she didn't know. The only thing that mattered was that he'd told her that he loved her. After dating six months, they decided to move in together. Lars was tired of living in the bland South Bay and wanted to move to the City. It was a dream for her— San Francisco had always been such a sparkling place where only those with money lived. Now she was living there. They married and bought a Victorian in Portrero Hill with a perfect view of the San Francisco skyline and easy access to the freeway. She got pregnant. She told herself that her child would not go without, as she had. She and her sister had never gotten anything extra. "If you don't need it, you shouldn't have it," her mother would say. They wore Wranglers and white t-shirts, white t-shirts and Wranglers. Her sister didn't care; she'd always been a cowgirl. But Sharon wanted dresses and mascara and purses—style, for God's sake. Sometimes she bought these things with her own money, but she hated dipping into her college fund. She didn't need a PhD in psychology to understand why she chose a husband who wasn't only a good man but was rich.

The vet was taking a long time. She thought that after five or ten minutes Dr. White would have come out to tell her that Muffin just had a cold and would be fine. How much could they be working on a hamster?

Sharon thought about being pregnant and her view of her career back then. She chuckled inside. She'd thought that once she had the kid, she'd hire a nanny. She wasn't about to lose her career to motherhood. Lars had been raised by a nanny, and he had turned out fine. The first day back at Google after her maternity leave, the nanny called her at 10:00 to tell her that Lily wouldn't stop crying. She felt the pull. Lily needed her. She had to be there for her baby. At lunch she told her boss that she had to quit, boxed up her desk, and drove 90 on Highway 280 to get home to Lily. Lars had encouraged her to quit before then. "It's not like we need the money," he'd said. In addition to his salary, they received $200,000 a year from his trust fund, and his parents had bought their house for them. Sharon had gotten used to the lifestyle—nice house, nice cars, designer clothes, organic food, spa treatments, white robe—but she couldn't get used to not working for it. Six years had passed, and it still didn't sit well. That they were rich because of her father-in-law's success in textiles felt wrong. Lars told her, "Relax and enjoy life." But she couldn't relax. She threw herself into motherhood, making sure she was there for Lily when she needed her. At first she thought it would only last while Lily was a baby, but how wrong she was! Her needs were always changing, and Sharon had to meet all of them. Providing Lily her favorite baby food turned into making sure Lily had her favorite solid food; going in to rock Lily every time she cried in the night became sleeping in her bed with her most nights; getting her a special pillow for her baby car seat became getting her a portable DVD player for the car.

Sharon stood up and stretched. She wandered to a display case holding pet bling—collars and leashes with sequins, Italian collar charms, large earrings. Lily sometimes pulled her into the neighborhood pet store and had her buy Muffin a CD for hamsters, organic hamster snacks, a hanging mirror, or a wool sleeping pad. It always made Lily so happy. Yet some days after getting Lily to school, as she was putting away Lily's collection of stuffed animals or folding her princess dresses or turning off her iPad, she wondered if all of it was necessary. She once had asked Lars if they should be giving Lily so many things. He looked up from reading the *New York Times*. "Why not let her have them? She's a kid."

"But shouldn't she have to earn them?"

"She'll have to work enough when she's an adult. Let her enjoy her childhood. It only happens once."

Sharon thought of last year's Christmas. Lily didn't receive a gift she really wanted—a Pillow Pet Dream Light. After opening her presents, she started to cry. "Where's my Pillow Pet Dream Light?" Sharon felt terrible. She'd bought all the other gifts on Lily's list, but stores had sold out of the Pillow Pet Dream Light before she could get one. Amazon couldn't get her one till after Christmas. She even had her mother check stores in Merced. No luck. Sharon still felt like she hadn't made Lily's Christmas perfect. She hugged the crying Lily.

"It was on my list, mommy. I wanted it more than those other dumb gifts."

"Don't worry, sweetie, we'll get you one this week."

"No, I want it now! *Today's* Christmas."

"We can't, sweetie; the stores are all closed."

"You're mean! I hate you!" Lily cried and ran to her room, slamming the door.

Sharon felt terrible. She went to Lily's door and knocked.

"Go away. I hate you!"

Sharon's parents were there that holiday, and her mother later pulled her aside in the kitchen.

"Maybe it's none of my business, but kids don't need more things when they have enough. You keep buying her everything she wants and babying her. You're spoiling her."

Sharon didn't want to hear it. Her parents had always been too tight to buy Sharon and her sister anything that wasn't absolutely *needed*. Even when the owner gave her father big bonuses at the end of harvest, her parents didn't get them anything special.

"Things are different now, mom."

"Oh, it's now okay to raise an asshole?"

"Lily's *not* an asshole."

"She will be if you keep spoiling her."

At first she dismissed her mother's comment, thinking she was ignorant of contemporary parenting. Yet she did fear Lily becoming someone who lived for shopping and material things and would be bitchy. She feared Lily wouldn't have true friends and wouldn't be able to stay married and wouldn't know how to be a good parent. But she and Lars wouldn't let that happen to Lily, would they? Sharon wondered what could be taking Dr. White so long. She pulled out her iPhone to check messages. There were a few: One from Lars saying his meeting at the London office had gone well; one from the coordinator of her book club; one from the caterer verifying the menu for Lily's birthday party.

Sometimes Sharon heard, "I hate you!" and it sounded like a train blaring its horn as it raced through an intersection. When she saw not one but three Pillow Pets on Lily's bed, she heard, "I hate you!" When she gave in to Lily's daily plea to stop at the bakery for a cream puff, she heard, "I hate you!" When she tied Lily's shoes for her even though she could do it herself, she heard, "I hate you!"

But what was she supposed to do? Lily wasn't growing up in an almond orchard outside a hick town. They lived in one of the most expensive, progressive cities in the country. Different culture. Kids were encouraged to express themselves more. They needed more help and attention. They needed affirmations that they were important. They needed to feel special. Otherwise their self esteem could suffer or be underdeveloped. Maybe the way she and Lars were raising Lily wouldn't fly in Merced, but that didn't make it wrong. It was just different. Still, Lily's comment chewed a hole from Sharon's inner ear to her stomach. How could Lily tell her that she hated her after all she'd given her, after all she'd done for her? Nearly four months had passed since that horrible experience, and Sharon still felt hollow when her mind replayed, "I hate you!"

The vet tech emerged. "Dr. White wants to talk with you in his office," she said without looking at Sharon.

It couldn't be good if he wanted to talk in his office, she thought. Sharon followed the tech down a hall decorated with framed photographs of schnauzer puppies, tabby kittens, brown bunnies, and brown and white hamsters. She entered Dr. White's office. He sat behind a large desk. His degrees hung on one wall. Two floor-to-ceiling windows on the other wall let in gray light from the foggy day. Sharon sat down and the tech walked out.

Dr. White folded his hands. "I'm sorry, but Muffin didn't make it."

Sharon stared at him, her mind skipping ahead to picking up

Lily. What would she tell her?

Dr. White went on. "Muffin had pneumonia. It's not uncommon for hamsters to come down with it. And when they do, they can rarely fight it off. I'm very sorry."

Sharon sighed. She pictured Lily wailing and screaming at her, "But you promised!" Maybe she could find another hamster that looked like Muffin. She could put Muffin's sweater on it and tell Lily that Dr. White had given Muffin some medicine and that he was all better. Lily didn't need to know what happened. It wasn't right for children to have to deal with death.

"We do provide a cremation service. Many families choose to purchase one of our memorial boxes. The receptionist can show you our selection, everything from hardwoods to silver to gold plated— they're very classy. Or, you could elect to lay Muffin to rest at Eternal Lawn, the pet cemetery in Daly City. We have their information."

She thought of Tiger, the tabby she had when she was a little girl. He slept with Sharon every night. One day a worker was speeding in his pickup down the dirt road in front of their house and ran over Tiger. He flew up into the air, end over end in a cloud of dust. The truck didn't stop. Sharon screamed and ran to him. He was bleeding from his mouth. He wasn't moving but his eyes were open.

Sharon's mother ran out of the house. "Damn him for speeding down this road!" She held Sharon from behind and rocked back and forth. "Oh baby girl, I'm sorry. I know you loved him."

"He's not dead, mama. Look, his eyes are open."

A small puddle of blood floated on top of the road.

"Poor Tiger's gone, baby girl." She squeezed Sharon tighter. "We can get you another kitty."

"I don't want another kitty. I want Tiger," she cried.

"I know, I know." Her mother held on to her. She watched the puddle of blood spread. "Unfortunately, everything dies, baby girl. It's hard, but it's part of life."

After Sharon stopped crying, her mother kneeled down to her. "We can't leave Tiger in the road, baby girl. We have to bury him."

"I don't want to, mama."

"That's all right. I'll take care of it."

Sharon went inside her room and sat on her bed. She kept seeing the image of Tiger flying into the air. She crept to the window. Her mother was digging a hole in the corner of their back lawn. When she finished she grabbed a square shovel and gently scooped up Tiger, dropped him into the hole, and started dumping dirt inside. Sharon ran outside.

"Mama, stop! Tiger's going to be trapped. He won't be able to get out!"

Her mother leaned on her shovel. "Baby girl, Tiger's dead now. He can't get out."

"But we have to give him a chance."

"I wish we could, baby girl."

Sharon remembered all of that pain. She saw the brown patch in the corner of the lawn and the bowls of food and milk she set next to it in the evening. She saw herself wake up and run outside the next day, only to see the brown patch and bowls unchanged. A couple of days later when she realized that Tiger wasn't coming back, the pain toppled on her like a landslide. She couldn't subject Lily to such a thing.

She didn't feel comfortable asking Dr. White if people buried pets in their yards. In Merced, sure, but not in San Francisco. What would she tell her friends who saw the brown patch in the corner of the back lawn, that it was Muffin's grave? They'd think she was Okie. They'd wonder why she would traumatize her child like that.

"Dr. White, is there any way to store Muffin's body until we make a decision? My husband's away, so we may need a few days."

"Not a problem. I fully understand. You can just let us know."

"Oh, and can I get Muffin's sweater?"

Dr. White raised his eyebrows. He paused and then said, "Sure, we can do that. We'll get it to you in the waiting room."

Sharon knew that her request made her look cheap, but she had to have the sweater. "Thank you," she said and walked out of the office.

In the waiting room, a man was petting his Persian cat and repeating, "You're my little cookie, Charlotte." The more Sharon thought about it, the more she liked her plan to purchase a new Muffin. She could find a hamster with basically the same markings, put the sweater on it, and all would be well.

The vet tech brought out the sweater and Muffin's carrier and handed them to Sharon. "Thanks," she said, and turned to leave. The man kept saying, "You're my little cookie."

*

Sharon drove toward the Stonestown Mall, where there was a Petco. She weighed the options: buy a new Muffin and make Lily believe it was the same hamster; have Muffin cremated and allow Lily to pick out the memorial box; have Muffin buried at Eternal Lawn. She needed Lars. She pulled over next to a small neighborhood park and texted him: "need help w/smthng. can u talk?"

Toddlers and small children scampered about the park's multicolored sheet of rubber covering the ground. She waited for Lars to text her back and watched the children and the parents, mainly mothers sitting on benches. Some kids were playing tag. They must have been three or four years old. The mothers wore fancy sweat suits and sunglasses.

Lars didn't text back. Sharon hated when she had to make big decisions without him. He always knew what to do. A boy on the playground tripped and fell. He sat up and didn't cry until his mother screamed, "Oh Micah!" and sprang from the bench. He bawled as she held him like a baby. Thank God his mother was right there. Sharon knew that if that had been her mother, she wouldn't have given the kid the time of day. One time a boy who lived near them in the country shot Sharon in the cheek with his BB gun. It felt like a hornet sting. She ran inside to her mother, who was ironing clothes. She grabbed Sharon's head and leaned in to have a look. "It's just a little red. You're fine. Now go tell Aaron that if he does that again, you'll break his arm." How could her mother have been so unsympathetic? But had she been totally wrong? Where was the perfect line between comforting and ruining a child? The mother of the boy who'd fallen pulled out a bag of M&Ms and gave him some. He shoved them in his mouth and held out his hands while still chewing. She poured him more.

Lars still didn't text. She started the car and drove toward the mall. It was her only good choice.

She pulled into the mall parking lot and checked her phone

again. Nothing. She texted Lars: "must talk call me!"

The Petco had many hamsters in different cages and tube complexes, running on wheels, eating, sleeping. Sharon leaned in close and looked at each one, her head bobbing among the cages like a buoy in the tide. Some had brown heads, but they weren't completely brown. Lily would know instantly. She checked her phone. Nothing from Lars. It was only 7:30 p.m. in London. What could he be doing? She only had an hour and a half before she had to pick up Lily. She walked to the front counter and asked an employee to call other stores for a hamster with a completely brown head. While the employee did that, Sharon checked her phone. Still nothing.

"Okay, I found a hamster that's white and brown without a speck of white on its head. It's at our store in the Stanford Mall."

"Great! Tell them to hold it for me. My name's Sharon." She ran out of the store.

As she opened her car door with her plan to replace Muffin on her mind, she heard, "I hate you." She ignored it and checked her phone. Nothing. "where r u???" she texted. She started the car. Luckily she was close to Highway 280. If she sped she might have just enough time to get there and back. She set her phone on her lap.

She drove along the road in front of the mall. The freeway entrance was a few blocks ahead. The fog was burning off. Patches of blue sky would appear and then get filled in by fog. Lars still hadn't called. She thought of moving an irrigation line one early fall evening. It was the first time she'd done it alone. She'd pick up a piece of hot aluminum pipe, walk it two rows over, attach it to the line, and then go for another piece. It was late enough in the day that soft light eased through the almond trees. She remembered being sweaty and dirty and her back aching, but something about it felt good. When she finished, she sat against a tree and drank from her water jug and looked at the lines of silver pipe she'd moved. She felt like she'd done something. It was a good feeling, one that made her happy all over, made her tingle in a wholesome way. She walked home through the orchard, sometimes stepping on fallen twigs, feeling that tingle. When would Lily get to feel that?

Sharon drove past rows of apartments surrounded by tall evergreens. She saw the sign: 280 South Right Lane. That was her on-ramp, but she took her foot off the gas pedal. Her mind told her to turn right, but she couldn't do it.

She looked at the highway entrance as she passed by and felt an odd sense of relief. She moved into the left lane and pulled into the left turn lane just as the green arrow illuminated. She did a U-turn and accelerated. The fog was very thin now. Sharon dropped her visor. She tossed her phone into the passenger's seat. She drove back across town, across Market Street, and finally up to Pacific Heights, to Dr. White's office.

The receptionist looked surprised to see her. "Hi, did you want to see the memorial boxes after all?"

A man with a shar pei walked in and stood behind her. He looked at his dog and said, "Sit, Bijan." The dog sat down.

Sharon looked at the receptionist. "No, I'd like to get Muffin's body."

"Oh." She looked at Sharon and blinked a couple of times. "We usually don't—Excuse me while I go ask Dr. White." She got up and walked down the hall.

The man patted the shar pei. The dog stood back up. "No, sit," the man said. The dog sat.

Sharon heard Dr. White's office door open. The receptionist walked back holding her mouth tight. She leaned over the counter and spoke low to Sharon. "Dr. White advised against taking Muffin right now. Muffin's body is completely frozen in a clear plastic bag." She added apologetically, "Sorry, it's how we keep bodies while families are deciding."

The shar pei whined and lay down on the ground.

Sharon pictured Muffin in the bag. She pictured showing it to Lily. It would upset her. It would be hard for both of them.

"That's okay," Sharon said. "I'd like to take it home."

# RED ROCK CANYON

It was just like Cara to blame me when she got stung by a scorpion.

When we were planning our road trip, she'd insisted we head straight to the Sierra, but I finally got her to agree to camp at Red Rock Canyon. The place was important to me. I'd spent seven days there one Christmas after breaking up with a woman who wanted to control my life. I was lonely at first, but every day I hiked through miles of blood red canyons and over wide open desert land that led to nowhere, and every evening I returned to my campsite tired and sore, my lips chapped, a few toes blistered. I came out the other side of that week feeling better and freer than I had in months. I'd always wanted to return, but Cara hated the desert, so we usually raced right by Red Rock when we were driving from Pasadena to ski at Mammoth or climb outside of Bishop or hike Whitney. No matter how much I talked up Red Rock Canyon and the Mojave, she didn't buy it, said it creeped her out—"It's where Charles Manson did some fucked up shit." So I guess I got lucky to get one night at Red Rock. "But we have to get out of there first thing in the morning," she'd said. I wanted to at least amble through some canyons, but I agreed to her condition. I guess sometimes you just have to take what you can get.

The night before she was stung, we had set up camp in a desert dust storm. I could tell she was pissed, but she didn't say anything. Wind shook our tent through the night, making it impossible to sleep and snapping a tent pole. Red dust snuck through tent zippers and turned our green sleeping bags pink, our faces red, and our teeth gritty, but the morning was calm and bright. Bees buzzed in nearby creosote bushes. Cara stuffed our sleeping bags while I broke down the tent.

"Cara, can you help me shake out the tent?" I asked.

She reached down to pick up a corner and then screamed and shook her foot.

"What happened?"

"Something just bit me! Get some ice!" She hobbled toward the picnic table.

I ran toward my Honda hoping Cara wouldn't lay into me for bringing us to Red Rock Canyon. "Did you see what it was?"

"It was big, and it flew away. I think it was a wasp."

"Are you sure? Should I grab your bee kit?"

"It wasn't a bee." She held her foot like a yogi and stared at her third toe. "There's no stinger. Will you just get me some ice?"

Cara propped her foot on the picnic table and set an ice pack on it. I rolled up the tent, thinking about her episode the year before. She didn't like to wear shoes when she dragged around the hose to water her native plants, potted basil, and sunflowers. Going barefoot apparently kept her feet tough for rock climbing. I wanted to tell her that something could bite or sting her, but telling Cara she's making a mistake isn't easy. I'd learned to avoid arguments by not saying much. Then it happened: One evening at dusk Cara was watering her plants when something nailed her foot. By the time she limped inside, hives were running up her legs. I almost felt good about it. That's what she got for walking around like Sacajawea. I nearly said something, but it wouldn't have made a difference. She thought her way was the only way of doing things. Just that night she'd lectured me on how to stack plates in the dish drain. The next evening she was out there again without shoes as if nothing had happened, and I was hoping something would nail her foot again.

Cara sat at the picnic table and iced her foot. I still expected her to curse me, but it didn't happen. I pulled the Benadryl from our first aid kit. The meds had expired a year before. Shit. I couldn't tell her. Before leaving on our trip, she had asked me if I'd updated the first-aid kit, and I'd said yes. We hadn't accessed it in over a year, so I didn't give it another thought. To overlook the Benadryl's expiration date was a rookie mistake, especially because I'm a nurse. She'd kill me if she knew.

"How do you feel, Cara?"

"My hands and feet are tingling."

"Do you want a Benadryl?"

"No, I don't want to fall asleep. I'll be all right."

"Any hives?"

"No. Let's go. We gotta get closer to our climb."

Our road trip had first taken us down the coast to surf in San Diego, and now we were heading up Highway 395 to climb some new routes on a nice slab of granite outside of Bishop. The place seemed perfect for us. I'd be able to grunt up some 5.9 routes, and Cara would skip up some 5.11s. It wasn't easy being the weaker climber, especially because she seemed to like it. Sometimes when I'd come off a hold or wasn't able to get over a crux, she'd cop a condescending tone and tell me what to do, even when other climbers were around. I'd try to ignore her and make the move on my own, but that usually got me nowhere, especially because I'd be fuming inside as she repeated, "Come on, climb with your legs, not your arms," or "Remember, move fast on those small holds." Her advice was always right and helped me top out, but I still wanted to tell her to just shut up. She always needed to tell me what to do. "Matt, don't drink so much coffee." "Matt, don't drive like my grandma." "Matt, hang your towel straight on the towel rack." I thought about packing my things and leaving her, even though we'd been together two years. But I'd always done that, walk away from relationships— the smallest problem with a girlfriend, and I was out of there. Before Cara, I'd never been with someone more than eleven months. I had to make this one work. I was 38 for God's sake. All my friends had been married for years and even had kids. It was time for me to figure it out.

I finished packing our camping gear and loaded up the car. Cara reclined her seat and elevated her calloused foot on the dusty dashboard. She nibbled on some cashews. She was a vegetarian because she felt it wasn't right to kill anything that had a face. To be honest, her vegetarianism was a pain in the ass. She insisted we have separate frying pans, baking pans, cutting boards, even serving spoons! To keep things simple, I agreed to go veggie on our road trips so that our cookware fit into a single milk crate.

We drove north into blue sky that wrapped around still Joshua trees and the brown lower end of the Sierra, right before the mountains go vertical and the real drama begins. Cara looked at the mountains on the left and the sagebrush desert on the right. She was quiet. That's how she was after getting injured, almost like she was dealing with some kind of defeat. So we drove up that two-lane part of 395 in silence, and she fell asleep. I paid attention to her breathing and at one point reached over and took her pulse, which was nice and calm at 50.

Before our trip we'd been fighting a lot. She didn't like that I sometimes went out for beers after work. I knew better than to go out with any female nurses, but what's wrong with enjoying a pint with the guys? It was a great way to come down off a shift, especially after being ordered around by asshole ER doctors for twelve hours. I'd call home to tell Cara, and she'd have that edgy tone that made me out to be a deadbeat boyfriend. When I'd get home, she'd ask me the same questions: Which bar'd you go to? Who was there? Did anyone else join you? Did you meet anyone? I'd calmly answer, but inside I'd be twisted up and would try to get to bed before an argument broke out, but that didn't always happen.

When we came to the Owens Valley, Cara woke up. I kept it at 55 so that we could take in the geological awe of the Sierra's east side. Cara pointed at snow-covered peaks cutting into the sky. "Great ice climbing in these parts." I had to hand it to her: she had guts I'd never have. On rock she lunged at holds the size of dimes, dangled from overhangs with two fingers, and often declined a belay just to feel the thrill of free climbing, knowing that one wrong move meant death. I didn't climb ice with her because the thought of it scared the shit out of me, but I belayed her. She drove in her ice axes like Ali pounding Frazier and kicked her spikes into the frozen wall like Bruce Lee busting up a concrete pillar. But if I didn't have the tension of the rope exactly the way she wanted it, she'd yell, "Tighter, damnit! Don't you know how to keep me tight?"

As we drove along I had her drink a lot of water to flush out her system. Every time I handed her the Nalgene bottle, she said, "I know, okay?" When Cara and I had gotten serious as a couple, I became Wilderness EMT certified. If she broke her clavicle from going ass over teakettle on her mountain bike, or dislocated her shoulder while glissading down Shasta, I wanted to know what to do out there. Other than my work buddies, Cara had replaced just about everyone in my life. I'd even grown apart from my family for a while. My mom pointed out that I hardly called them anymore. She was right. I'd dropped my connection with family down a notch. I used to talk with my brother throughout the week and my parents every couple days, but Cara said it was unusual. At first I got defensive, and then she said that we were all codependent. I'd never thought that. Maybe she was right. I told my mom, and all hell broke loose. "You're going to listen to a woman you've dated five months?" I did, and for a while it brought Cara and me closer. But lately I'd been sneaking calls to my family. When Cara left to run errands, I'd watch her back out of the driveway and then run to the phone to call my parents or brother. I wanted to spend last Christmas with my family, but Cara said that it would make her uncomfortable because she felt judged by them. She'd never even tried to get to know them, but I guess I can't argue with her feelings. She never visited her family in Vegas. She said they didn't have anything in common.

A few times during the drive Cara mentioned her tingling hands and feet and that she felt nauseated. But her pupils weren't dilated, her pulse wasn't pounding, and her color wasn't missing. By the time we crept into Lone Pine and parked across the highway from Mt. Whitney, her symptoms had faded and she was dying for a frosty.

We drove down the town's short main drag that was part nineteenth century western, part 1950's Americana. Near the edge of town was Lone Pine Frosty. I parked under a cottonwood.

"Do you want to eat it in the car?" I asked.

"That'd be great. Make it vanilla."

I went to the window. A blond teenage girl took my order, rang me up, and handed me the frosty. Things were turning around for Cara. She had her energy back and was in a good mood. Our trip was back on track.

I returned to the car and handed her the frosty. She stared at me, her eyebrows pressing down on her face.

"What?" I asked.

"What was that about?"

"What?"

"The way you were looking at that girl."

"Huh?"

"I saw you looking at her. Jesus, Matt, right in front of me. And she's probably sixteen." She bit off the frosty's pointed top and turned away.

She did this sometimes, accused me of checking out other women. It always ended in a fight. How couldn't it? I'm not perfect, but I don't have a wandering eye. The last time Cara accused me of this—for supposedly being too friendly with a checker at Safeway— we got into it and didn't talk for two days. After our fights, I usually couldn't take the cold tension. I'd apologize first so that we could move on. Last year when I was in therapy, my therapist had suggested that I not give in so quickly, but I had to this time. An argument would ruin our trip.

I waited for Cara to say something, but she didn't. She finished the vanilla part and started in on the cone, taking a big bite. She chomped the thing like a wolf pulverizing the bones of an innocent rabbit. I hated her right then. Her aggressive ways, she was always lashing out at me and talking down to me. She was always so sure about everything. The muscles on the sides of her face flexed and her jaw worked up and down, and then she swallowed the big bite all at once and attacked the cone again with her big teeth. She chewed with her mouth open like the animal that she was. I couldn't even look another woman in the eye anymore without her yelling at me for being a womanizer. Me, a womanizer? I'd never tried to pick up a woman. I didn't even know any pick-up lines. I should have opened the car door and run, caught a bus back home, and left her, but I sat there and let the accusation hover in the air. She pushed the rest of the cone into her mouth and grinded it down, a few pieces even flying out of her mouth, and then swallowed it all in one gulp. She ran her tongue around the rim of her mouth and turned toward me. "Are you done staring?"

I took a breath and pushed down my anger.

"So are we going to that campsite or what?" she asked.

I started the car.

Cara had read about a BLM campground three miles north of Independence. I got us back on the road and drove north feeling weak and pathetic. I kept seeing the image of myself running from the car, leaving her, but each mile I drove the image got farther and farther away. Ten miles later we hit Independence, which was a lot like Lone Pine but had a high school and a small hospital.

Our campsite sat along a swollen creek lined by oaks. Finches played in some willows. Jagged, snow-covered peaks exploded out of a sea of sage. Shades of pink and lavender streaked across the evening sky. Something opened up inside of me that took away my anger. Or maybe all that beauty tamped it all down. Either way, those feelings seemed gone, as if the creek had washed them away. Cara and I glanced at each other and smiled big. She saw all of the beauty and felt it too. Nature was bringing us back together. The cold air was so fresh that it smelled sweet. Our eyes watered. We threw on fleece jackets and started to bust a move to set up camp. I laid down the tarp and pulled out the tent. Cara snapped together tent poles. Our trip was back on track. This was a new beginning. I imagined us later sparking a fire and cuddling up next to it and sharing stories and planning our day of climbing. We'd look up at the blanket of twinkling stars every once in awhile and feel our connection to the cosmos and to each other. Then we'd bed down in our cozy tent, and hopefully have make-up sex.

Cara reached down to clip a pole into the tent but jumped back, letting out a skull-cracking scream. She shook her hand. "Something just stung me! There's an animal in there!"

I rushed to her.

She cradled her hand and was on the verge of crying. "There's something in there!"

I turned and looked down. A neon green scorpion faced us

from under some tent mesh. Five inches long. Stinger cocked back. Pincers flared out and pointing up.

"Oh God, it's a scorpion," Cara said. "That's what got me before."

"How do you know?"

"Because my hands and feet are tingling again." She took two steps backwards. I thought she was going to pass out, so I moved to catch her, but she planted her feet, stood up straight, and turned toward me. "You rolled it up in the tent!"

"Huh?"

"Are you deaf? You rolled it up in the tent this morning!"

"Oh shit." I pictured myself rolling up the tent, not knowing that the scorpion was trapped inside. "I didn't mean to. I had no idea. I thought a wasp tagged you."

"You and your Red Rock Canyon! You just had to go there! You rolled the scorpion up in the tent at fucking Red Rock Canyon!"

"I know, but I didn't mean to."

"Well you did! You just had to go to Red Rock Canyon. Now kill it!"

"Huh?"

"Kill it, damn you, kill it!"

I didn't know what to do, but I wanted her off me, so I ran to the car to grab something to use to kill it, but I didn't know what to grab. I didn't want to kill the scorpion. It hadn't done anything wrong. This whole thing wasn't its fault. It was just an innocent creature trying to survive, doing what it had to do to fend off something bigger than itself. But if I didn't kill it, I'd never hear the end of it. So much for not killing something that had a face. I pulled the aluminum frying pan from the milk crate and ran back.

Cara was pale. The scorpion still faced us, ready to defend itself. I raised the pan and then paused.

"Are you kidding me?" Cara yelled. "Kill the fucking thing! It stung me!"

My stomach hurt. I knew I was making a mistake. I slammed the poor thing with the frying pan, smashing it hard. It didn't move. It was definitely dead, but I raised the pan and smashed it again. Then I did it again, and again. Cara yelled, "Okay, it's dead! You can stop now!" But I didn't stop. I smashed it, and then smashed it again and again. "Just stop!" Cara yelled. I kept smashing it until the pan was bent in two and the scorpion was nothing but bits of green mash. Then I turned and hurled the pan into the sea of sage brush.

Twilight was dropping its curtain fast. The colors in the sky had faded into a dull gray that would soon be black. I knew I needed to get Cara to the hospital. I didn't know how much scorpion venom her body could take in a single day. The expired Benadryl was probably worthless, though I could have given her a couple for a sense of security. But I didn't.

Cara held her hand like a baby and stared at me. It seemed like she wanted me to do something. The light was nearly gone, and the cold was settling in, but I didn't move.

# THE QUIET TIME

The closest gas station was on 9th Street, and 9th Street meant prostitutes, meth, and stabbings. When I pulled in, no one was around except for a turbaned Indian man standing behind the register in the kiosk. No stars or moon out, just the station's buzzing fluorescent lights and a bare bulb hanging above the man in the kiosk. A few dead street lamps lined the cracked and pitted road flanked by beat up industrial storefronts and a junkyard.

I didn't want to go to the station that night. Since my dad's death two weeks before, I'd wanted to stay close to my wife and new baby. I was okay when I was delivering medical supplies, but once I turned off the truck for the day and darkness came, I wanted to be at home. Kathy hadn't lost a parent yet, so she didn't understand what I was going through. Most nights we'd sit on the couch, and she'd run her hand through my hair while laughing at reruns of *Seinfeld* that I couldn't get into. But just being with her and the baby made me feel less jumpy.

For three days I'd flaked on checking my tires because I barely had enough time to make all of my deliveries. My boss, Kirk, had written me up once before for driving on low tires. One more of those and I'd be out of work for five days. I couldn't let that happen. Some months we could barely pay the rent. Without dad we didn't need a three-bedroom house, but I wasn't ready to move to another place. Kirk snuck around in his silver, bullet-shaped Ford Taurus and spied on us drivers. I'd rolled the dice for three days by not checking my tires, and it was pestering me like a fly buzzing around my head. And my truck was below a quarter tank. Kathy told me to wait till morning, but mornings were tough because I'd been having a hard time getting out of bed. I couldn't trust that I'd be able to deal with gas-station crap before loading my truck at 6:00 a.m. So before some cop show sucked me in, I got off the couch, put on my father's down jacket, and headed out, mad at myself for putting it off so long.

I began to fill up my truck. A low-rider pulled in blaring rap music. A big guy with a shaved head and Fu Manchu muscled his way across the open pavement toward the kiosk. He slapped down a bill and said, "Gimme ten on three." My heart beat in my throat. I squeegeed my windshield and kept my eyes on the glass as his rap music screamed, "Fuckin' bitch" this, and "Fuckin' cop" that.

Fu Manchu yanked the nozzle and jammed it into his car. I looked at the Indian man. He was busy reading the newspaper. Fu Manchu soon finished gassing up, slammed the nozzle into the pump, and screeched his way out of the station, heading the wrong way down a one-way street. I was glad that he was out of the picture. Now I just had to fill my tires in the dark corner of the lot next to the alley, and I'd be out of there.

I measured a rear tire's pressure and was about to shoot air into it when a short black woman holding a big garbage bag walked around the back end of my truck, making me jump. "Excuse me, sir," she said, "but I just got off the bus, and I need a little help."

She was older—maybe fifty-five. She kept her distance. I looked around for her partner—someone who'd flash a blade, grab my wallet, and steal Kirk's truck. But I didn't see anyone else.

"I'm alone," she said.

Maybe she was, but I wasn't about to trust anyone in that part of town. I needed to fill those damn tires and get out of there.

"I don't have any extra money," I said, turning away.

"I don't need money. I need help. I just got off the bus, and I'm tired. I just need a ride to Carver Street. You look like a nice man."

I didn't look up. "My wife and baby are at home, and I need to get back."

"Please, sir, I'm tired, and I don't know how I'll make it those couple miles. And I don't know who might be out—"

"This is a company truck, and I can't carry unauthorized passengers," I said, sounding unsure of myself instead of official, like Kirk. I wasn't lying. One time I had to deliver two canisters of O2 to an older man with COPD. He and his wife lived two blocks from the hospital. When I pulled up, his wife ran out and said, "Hurry!" I ran in and saw the little man clutching his barrel chest. I told his wife to call 911. She did and then begged me to take him to the hospital.

"I'm sorry, ma'am, but my company won't allow me to."

"But we can get him there faster!" she screamed. "He might die!"

She was right, but Kirk had said *under no circumstances*, so I didn't. I felt rotten.

But in the last three months of dad's life I broke that rule a lot. Every week I'd map out routes that made it easy for me to swing by our house to take him for dialysis. He'd sit down low. Every time I spotted a silver Ford Taurus, I'd say "Duck!" and he'd put his head down. But his Fedora hat would stick up, and we'd both laugh. I was lucky that Kirk never caught me. I wasn't about to push my luck with this stranger.

I pressed the adapter into the tire valve. She walked away real slow, and I was glad.

A stranger on 9th Street at 9:15 p.m. was bad news. She could have had a knife in her coat. And what was in that bag? I did the right thing by following Kirk's rule. But Mike came to mind: *We're here to help each other.* Mike and I had grown up together. After high school he went away to a couple of big universities and got educated and then came back to marry his sweetheart and teach at the local college. He still liked to hang out with me. My other friends who'd gotten fancy degrees had stopped returning my calls. Not Mike. We'd go out for beers, and sometimes after a few pints we'd talk about life. Lately I'd been watching some ants near our front porch. They knew exactly what to do, all of them tooling along, knowing their purpose, and I wondered what *our* purpose was. I asked Mike at the pub one night. He didn't even have to think about it.

"We're here to help each other." He looked at me, nodded once, and took a swig of his IPA.

I thought about it for a second. "It's that simple, isn't it?"

"Yep."

Sometimes when I'd be driving or doing random stuff I'd hear Mike's words. But I couldn't trust some stranger in that part of town. I read the paper and watched the news—I knew about all the crime on 9th Street. But the little woman seemed harmless. What could she do to me? But was she really alone? And did she have anything in her coat or in that bag? I finished filling my tires, jumped in the truck, and drove out of the station.

"Okay, I'll make you a deal," I said to myself. "If you see her on your way home, you'll pick her up. Fuck your worries, and fuck Kirk. She's alone and can barely move. If you don't see her, you'll go home."

Two blocks later, there she was—hunched over, wobbling down the street. I pulled over and swung open the door. She grunted as she got in.

"Thank God. Oh bless you," she said. "Oh I didn't know how I's going to make it. I thought I'd just walk some and stop and rest, but I'm scared out here at night." She put the bag on her lap and wrapped her arms around it, her wrinkled hands pulling it toward her like a kid does a big stuffed animal. She only had a few teeth. Her skin was very black, and her eyes were black. She never looked at me. She looked down the long stretch of 9th Street beyond some warehouses, where a dirty motel's half-lit sign blinked.

"So you just got off a bus?" I eased the clutch back slow so that the truck wouldn't jerk.

"Yeah. Just got back from Oakland. Went there to visit my sister."

"Yeah?" I shifted into second.

"Uh huh."

I shifted into third and kept it at 25 miles per hour. Nobody was on the road. It seemed like we were the only ones out at all.

"Just needed some company, that's all," she said.

"Yeah?"

"Uh huh." She paused for little while. "My husband died a month ago of a heart attack."

We came to an empty intersection with a red light hanging over it. I sighed and downshifted.

"I'm sorry to hear that." I pressed on the brakes, and we stopped. "My dad died two weeks ago."

"Oh, I'm sorry about that. What'd he die of?"

"His kidneys gave out. Then his body just shut down."

"That's too bad."

The light turned green. I took off slowly and eventually shifted into second. I thought about dad at the dialysis center. I'd walk in with him and get him situated in one of those cushy chairs next to a machine that cleaned his blood. He'd set his hat on his lap, and Stephanie, his favorite nurse, would push clear tubes into the port near his neck and turn on the machine. I'd kiss dad on the cheek and tell him I'd pick him up real soon. I always looked back before leaving, and he'd raise his hand like an Indian chief. I'd wave back and then walk out into an overcast day, my heart hurting the whole time. I'd take the long way to my deliveries so that I could stop crying and wipe my eyes dry before wheeling an oxygen tank into a medical building or pulling up to somebody's house to take away an oxygen machine no longer needed because the person had died.

We drove past the motel with the half-lit sign.

"I took my dad to dialysis three times a week," I said.

"How long did he go to that?"

"Just a few months until other problems took over."

I kept it in second and drove well under the speed limit. I didn't shift into third. She interlaced her fingers and looked straight ahead.

I pictured dad's face the morning he died. The doctor had told me that he wouldn't make it through the night, so I stayed with him in the hospital, like he'd done with me in my room after mom died. In the morning he was still breathing, but it was rough, and his arms were bruised from all the IVs. I knew that he was going, but it didn't seem like it. Some slats of sunlight were lighting up his face, and he looked so calm and comfortable that I didn't believe that anyone could die looking so good. But his breathing got real ragged, and then it was like someone flipped the switch. The monitor screamed, and the little color his face still had started to fade. The nurse came in. She knew about dad's DNR order. She turned off the monitor. "Take as long as you want," she said and walked out.

I sat there a long time, until an orderly came in later and said, "Let me get that sun out of your eyes." He pulled on a chain that fully closed the blinds, taking the light out of the room.

The truck engine whirred, I took a couple of deep breaths, the woman blinked a few times. I didn't shift up. I wanted her place to be fifty miles away so that we could ride like that for a long time. We didn't say anything. Both of us looked ahead at the deserted street in front of us.

I turned onto Carver.

"How are you doing with it?" I asked.

"It's hard, you know, especially when I get home and he's not there. I still got his things. His slippers are next to the door. It's real hard."

I thought of my dad's room at our house. I saw his clothes still hanging in his closet and his sweatshirts above them and his shoes piled under them, and his shoe-shine kit in the corner and the loosely organized nature of it all and how it reflected my father's way of storing things. He had to still be there because all his things were still in his closet just as he'd left them. But when I pictured his bed and how smooth it looked, and didn't see the foam wedge that kept him propped up, or the oxygen tube running across the room, and didn't see the *Reader's Digest* or box of Kleenex on the nightstand or the used tissues on the floor, I saw that it wasn't the same, that it was all too neat for him to be there.

She lifted a crooked finger and pointed. "That's my apartment building right there on the corner." It was a bland stucco building with a few drooping junipers out front. "All this way you brought me. Thank God. I didn't know how I was going to make it."

I pulled over.

"This's fine right here." She reached for the door latch.

"Can I carry your bag inside for you?"

She turned toward me. Her eyes were kind. The sides of her mouth went up enough. She knew why I was asking.

"I appreciate that, son, but this's quiet time. It's hard, but quiet time's good."

I nodded. I felt lonely.

She slowly opened the door. "Thank you so much." She grunted as she stood up and closed the door like it was a piece of china. I watched her labor on. I pictured her opening her door and seeing her husband's slippers, and stepping into an empty home. I thought about what Mike had said. He was right. Two cars passed and disappeared around a corner. The road was clear, but I sat there in the idling truck, my foot on the brake.

# WAITING

Carol arrives a half hour early and circles the block for fifteen minutes until an SUV pulls away from the parking space she wants, the one kitty-corner to the Italian café. She inches her new BMW into the spot, careful not to scrape the wheels against the curb. Gray clouds hang over Sacramento. Broadway's four lanes buzz with passing cars, buses, and bicycles. Bundled-up pedestrians enter and exit cafés, galleries, bookstores, and boutiques. Carol unbuckles her seat belt but stays in the car. She watches the Italian café.

Two weeks before, Carol had called Brigitte to catch up. When she mentioned her upcoming show in Sacramento, Brigitte insisted that she drive from Fresno to see her.

"Don't bother. It's too far."

But Brigitte was adamant. "The baby is a month old, and you two still haven't met each other. We'll drive up to Sac when you're there."

Carol hasn't been able to fit a trip to Fresno into her schedule. Before this show in Sacramento, she had most recently accompanied her paintings to galleries in La Jolla and Taos. She pulls a pint of Häagen-Dazs vanilla from a paper bag and peels off the lid. Her spoon glides over the top layer like a skier making fresh tracks. When

Carol looks up, she sees Brigitte with her baby walking down the sidewalk toward the Italian café. Carol sits lower in her seat, just enough to see over the steering wheel. She hasn't told Brigitte that after she and Seth divorced, she'd gone a bit crazy and bought a new car. She absolutely loves it. Hauling around her paintings had always forced her to own bulky vehicles—a Land Cruiser, a Suburban, an Escalade. Once she could afford to hire others to transport her art, she was free to drive something smaller. Why not get a little red convertible? She deserved it. The car drives fine, but she mostly likes the way it looks—clean, sharp lines, rich red color perfectly complemented by a black top and leather interior. Driving it makes her feel sexy. She loves the looks she gets, especially when the top's down. Carol watches Brigitte, walking with such relaxed confidence, as if she's a seasoned local. Very Brigitte. She holds her newborn like she's been a mother for four years, not four weeks. Brigitte has cut her dark hair short. With her dainty face, she can get away with it. She's as petite as ever. Her pregnancy weight probably melted off of her in a week. After having Cory it took Carol a year of Weight Watchers and workouts with a personal trainer to lose some of her pregnancy weight. She's still carrying an extra twenty-five. Most mornings she looks in the mirror at her bulbous hips and rhino thighs, and she hates herself for it. After nights of pigging out she avoids mirrors altogether. Carol takes small bites of ice cream and watches her friend, whose French skin still has color, even in November. Hers is just dark enough not to burn, unlike Carol's freckled skin.

Carol takes in Brigitte's classic French style: a black leather bag hanging from her shoulder, a light rain coat, mid-cut boots, and a slim tan linen skirt. All are much more conservative than the flowery prints she wore when the two had met twelve years before at the Art Academy. Carol had instantly liked her. She was friendly and had a wonderful lightness about her. Brigitte had just moved to Berkeley from Paris with that bum. What was his name? Danny. Her first husband, the mangy drummer whose band was always on the verge of getting a break. Thank God she hadn't gotten pregnant with *his* baby.

When Brigitte reaches the Italian café, she stops and looks inside at the glass display case of pastries and gelato. She turns, searches the faces of people sitting at some outdoor tables, and walks inside. A moment later Brigitte comes back outside, glances again at the people at the tables, and looks up and down the sidewalk and across the street. Carol's spoon stops. Brigitte's not the type to pay attention to cars she doesn't know, but Carol still holds her breath. When Brigitte turns and adjusts the blanket around her baby, Carol exhales and takes another bite. Brigitte pulls out her phone and dials.

Carol's phone rings. She looks at her cell, sees Brigitte's number, and waits a minute before retrieving the message: "Hi *mon ami*. I'm here at Café Forenza. I'm going to order an espresso. If you want me to order you something, give me a call. See you soon!" Carol always marveled at her boundless generosity. Brigitte used to bring coffee and croissants to their studio classes, even when she worked for minimum wage at the bead store, after her divorce. It took finding Danny in bed with a drunk teenager for Brigitte to finally leave the bum, but at least she left him.

Carol eats more ice cream and lets the spoon sit in her mouth as she watches Brigitte sit down at one of the outdoor tables and pick up a conversation with a tall waiter in a white apron. The two nod and laugh. Carol has always envied Brigitte's ability to create rapport with complete strangers. It must have boosted sales when she sold hemp bracelets, necklaces, anklets, and toe rings at craft shows and music festivals. Her personality coupled with her French accent was irresistible. While Brigitte was out selling her hippie jewelry after they graduated, Carol was proving herself in the City. She had turned down her parents' offer to work for their Oakland-based shipping company. She wanted to make it on her own, to show them that she could carve out a life as an artist. She didn't have any trouble. An agent signed her on and got her large abstract oil paintings into a small gallery in the City's Mission District. Word about her art's bold colors and use of large shapes got around. The *San Francisco Chronicle* wrote a favorable review of Carol's work, comparing her use of color and shapes to that of Rothko. Her paintings started to fill lobbies in San Francisco skyscrapers and moved around the financial district like a doctor making rounds. CEOs, CFOs, stock brokers, and investment bankers bought her work for their big homes in Pacific Heights, Russian Hill, and the Marina. It became the norm for her to sell at least two paintings a month. Her paintings ranged from seven to ten thousand apiece, as much as Brigitte made in a year. One fall Carol finished a new body of work that resembled huge bar codes, and her agent lined up a show in the lobby of the Wells Fargo Building. Carol arranged to hang after hours, thinking nobody would be in the building to interrupt her. Downtown was wonderfully dead when she got there sometime after 10:00. She was in the middle of positioning a piece when a man came out of an elevator and stopped to look at her paintings.

"That's what it all comes down to, doesn't it?"

"Excuse me?" Carol turned and looked at him. He was dressed like all the men who worked downtown, but unlike the others he wasn't a suit. He was different. His hair was shaggy and his dark goatee wasn't sculpted. He wore a small, thin hoop earring. He had a leather messenger bag, not a briefcase.

"The bar codes. That sums up American culture. It's brilliant."

Carol made sure not to smile too much, but she beamed inside. "Do you work here?"

Seth worked in hedge funds. He asked for her number and he called a week later, just when Carol started to give up hope. She hadn't been in a relationship for over two years. Seth didn't knock her socks off, but he was...interesting. He was a groovy guy working in a high-powered job. And if he worked in hedge funds, he had to be loaded. Not that she needed to be with a rich man, but it certainly made Seth more attractive. They started having drinks at the Fairmont. He was always late—sometimes up to 30 minutes. It bugged Carol, but he was so mellow about everything that Carol thought she should lighten up, just let it slide. She wasn't about to complain to him about it, even when they started going out to dinner throughout the week. Then they started spending weekends at B&Bs in Big Sur, Sonoma, Mendocino. Carol loved that Seth opened his wallet, but it seemed that he was never one hundred percent present. He couldn't break free from his laptop and iPhone, always had a spread sheet to work on, a client to talk to. Carol thought she'd fix Seth's flakiness once they got married. She'd help him reprioritize. But he didn't. She knew he was a good husband (he bought her the house she wanted in Pacific Heights, didn't object to how she decorated it, wasn't the type to cheat on her), but he didn't give her the attention she wanted. After dinner he'd retreat to the den to work on his laptop or watch CNN. When Cory came along, he didn't change his routine, though once in a while he changed a diaper or pushed the baby in the stroller to the bagel shop.

Brigitte sets her espresso on the table and looks at each passerby. The baby starts to squirm. Carol can't remember its name, but she knows it's a boy. She eats two bites of ice cream, thinking about what she'll do when she sees the baby up close. Brigitte rocks the baby, but the baby continues to squirm. She remembers Cory squirming and squawking in public and her fear of others glaring at her. Brigitte hangs her bag on the other chair, casually opens her blouse, and drapes a white blanket over her chest and the baby. She makes breast feeding among a dozen strangers look easy. Carol never had the nerve to nurse Cory in public. She always ran to some bathroom to nurse on a toilet, hoping Cory would finish fast. But Cory never finished fast, so she stopped breast feeding him and turned to formula. The bottle was much easier, and she didn't have to worry about being embarrassed when her milk leaked though her silk blouses.

A city bus honks at a bicyclist, making Carol drop the Haagen-Dazs. Some melted ice cream pours onto the black floor mat. "Shit!" She rights the carton and grabs some wipes. She cleans it up, places the carton between her legs, and looks up.

Brigitte is still nursing the baby. She looks so mature, even wise, calmly sitting there with her child, waiting. Perhaps moving to Fresno and marrying Josh has finally grounded her. A few years back Carol had been worried about Brigitte. Over a four year period she lived with three different men—a line cook in the Haight, a blacksmith in Berkeley, and a pot head in Sausalito. Carol and Seth always included her and her men at holidays, even after the infamous 1998 Christmas at their home, when after dinner Brigitte's Che Guevara boyfriend pulled out a joint in front of Carol's parents. Carol looked at Brigitte, who leaned over and whispered, "Not here." Che put away the joint, but Carol's parents still excused themselves and left. Even then Carol didn't tell Brigitte to ditch the loser. She always patiently listened to Brigitte's complaints about her boyfriends and only shared her views when Brigitte asked.

In those years Brigitte would retreat to Carol and Seth's. Carol and Brigitte would stay up late and talk—about Brigitte's decision to settle in the US instead of France, about her boyfriends, about her financial struggles. Carol often slipped a few twenties into Brigitte's purse and always played dumb when Brigitte thanked her. Then Brigitte was hired to teach art at a charter school in the Mission. Carol liked that Brigitte had chosen to pursue a job that provided some stability. Josh was the school's Vice Principal. Brigitte started dating him and brought him over to meet Carol and Seth. Thank God he was normal. When he took a job as principal at a K-8 in Fresno, Brigitte moved with him. Carol couldn't imagine living *there*, but at least Brigitte had found a comfortable life. Brigitte had visited Carol once after she became pregnant, but that was many months ago. Since Brigitte had the baby, Carol had hardly heard from her. When they did talk, it was hard to hold a conversation because of the baby noises in the background. Carol remembers how it was.

It starts to sprinkle. Drops tap on the car's canvas roof and speckle the windshield. Carol leans forward. Brigitte gets up and goes next door into the bookstore, to the section nearest the window. Carol knows the store. Brigitte is looking at travel books. In their last phone conversation, Brigitte had mentioned that during spring break they were going to Buenos Aires. Seth had wanted to travel to England when Cory was a baby, but Carol wouldn't allow it—too many infections on planes and odd illnesses in foreign countries, she'd argued. But the real reason was that she couldn't fathom flying for twelve hours with a child and hundreds of people glaring at her every time Cory squawked. And here Brigitte was going to take her baby to the bottom of South America. She has always been careless, like when she rode to LA on the back of a biker guy's chopper. Carol sinks her spoon into the vanilla and leaves it there.

A light rain begins to fall. Passersby hurry along with their heads down or under umbrellas. Cars whiz by, spraying water from their tires. A bicyclist in a yellow slicker passes slowly. Carol makes out Brigitte next to the store window. She's holding her phone to her ear. Carol's phone rings. She waits. A minute later she accesses the message: "Hi *mon ami*. I'm still here, but I'm now in the bookstore.

Hope you're okay. See you soon!" Carol sets down the phone and leans forward again. Brigitte is still in the window, now looking out. The baby's head is exposed. Its hair is dark, not red like Cory's. Carol dressed Cory in a lot of white and black clothes to accentuate the richness of his red hair. It had a beautiful wave in it that softened when he took his baths. He had to have a bath every night before bed. As Cory would splash around in the tub, Carol read on the toilet and Seth answered emails or watched CNN in the den.

Big rain drops now fall and run down Carol's windshield, making everything blurry. She can still make out Brigitte as she steps out from the bookstore and stands under the awning, holding her baby close to her and rocking. Lines of water run off the awning.

One night as Cory played with his bubble boat in the tub, Carol's agent called to discuss a potential sale. She couldn't hear over Cory's motorboat sounds. She ran to the den, where Seth was staring into his laptop.

"Babe, I need to take this call from Malcom. Go sit with Cory, okay?"

"Okay."

Five minutes later she hung up and returned to the bathroom. Cory was face down in the tub. His hair was floating the way grass does in still water. "Cory? Cory! Cory!" She pulled his wilted body from the water and yelled, "Call 911, Seth! Call 911!" She laid Cory on the bath mat. His freckled face was pale, his lips blue. Carol remembered the CPR class she'd taken when she was pregnant, remembered the instructor saying, "Stay calm." She bent down next to Cory's mouth. No breath. She placed two fingers on his lower sternum and started chest compressions. A line of water dribbled out of the side of his mouth. Good sign, she thought. Seth yelled into the phone, "732 Gough! In Pac Heights! Yes, 732!" Carol pumped and more water dribbled from Cory's mouth. God did he take in a lot. She put her ear to his mouth. Still no breath. She gave him two quick breaths and started pumping his chest again. Seth came to the bathroom. "Oh my God." He stood over her with his hands on his knees. Beads of sweat formed on her forehead and upper lip. She was getting tired. Her shoulders ached, and her knees hurt, but she couldn't stop. She watched Cory's face. He was still pale. "It's okay, baby. It's okay." Water stopped coming out of Cory's mouth. His breath had to be coming. She put her ear to Cory's mouth but didn't feel his breath. She watched his chest. It didn't rise and fall. She gave him mouth to mouth and started pumping again. Sirens wailed from down the hill. Sweat covered her face. Her arms felt like they'd fall off, but she couldn't stop. Seth sprinted out into the street and waved his arms. Drops of sweat fell from Carol's nose on to Corry's chest. She pumped. Her eye sockets filled. "Come on, baby! Come on!"

Three paramedics rushed in with a body board. One took over the chest compressions while the other probed Cory's neck for a carotid pulse. "No pulse. Let's load him." One paramedic continued pumping his chest as the other two log rolled Cory onto the board and carried him to the ambulance. A paramedic waved Carol in. The ambulance screamed down San Francisco hills and through intersections. One paramedic asked Carol questions about Cory. The others pumped his chest and hooked him up to the AED. "No rhythm. I'm starting an IV of Epi."

Carol rubbed Cory's limp hand, repeating, "Wake up, baby, wake up."

The AED lit up. "We got a heartbeat."

"Oh, thank God. That's it, baby," Carol said.

Color started to return to Cory's face.

In the PICU at the hospital, Carol held Cory's hand. There were tubes everywhere. A catheter tube wound out the side of his bed, an IV tube ran to his arm, and a fat ventilator tube snaked into his mouth. The sound of the machine pumping air into and pulling it out of Cory filled the room. Carol watched his little chest rise and fall over a lifeless body.

Seth apologized to Carol, but she couldn't look at him. He apologized to Cory too, standing over his bed, tears running along the edges of his goatee, as he repeated, "I'm sorry, Cory. I'm sorry, Cory." The breathing machine droned in the background like an airplane stuck on the tarmac.

Brigitte came to the hospital. She sat next to Carol and held her hand. Doctors and nurses were in and out of the room around the clock. Cory's heart was beating fine, but he couldn't breathe on his own. The ventilator still did 100 percent of the work. Carol watched his chest rise and fall and kept an eye on his face. He looked so good with all the color in his freckled cheeks. He must be sleeping. He couldn't really need that machine if he looked like he did when he slept at home, could he? She wanted to pull the tube from his mouth to let him sleep normally. He would wake up. She just had to wait.

At the end of the week, a female doctor came in, sat down next to Carol, and looked at her with sad eyes. "It doesn't look like Cory has any brain function. Without the ventilator he's unable to breathe." She paused. The machine seemed louder. "You'll have to let us know what you want to do. I'm very sorry." Brigitte squeezed Carol's hand, but Carol didn't respond. She didn't believe the doctor.

Carol and Seth decided to turn off the machine the following day. Carol knew that Cory would be fine, that he'd start breathing on his own.

The next day the doctor turned off the machine and a nurse pulled the tube from Cory's mouth. The room went silent. Cory seemed smaller. Carol and Brigitte stood on one side of the bed, Seth stood on the other. They watched Cory. Carol stroked his hair. "Come on, baby." Carol waited to hear him cough once or twice and start breathing and open his eyes. She waited, staring at his face as the color faded from it, and it returned to the pale it wore when she'd pulled him from the tub.

Seth covered his face with his hands and started to cry. Brigitte wrapped her arms around Carol, but Carol didn't respond. She still stared at Cory, waiting. The doctor and nurse left the room and closed the door. Carol still stared at Cory as she started to shake her head and wail, "No! No!"

After the funeral Carol's stomach was so hollow and her chest so full of rage that she couldn't talk to Seth, even about mundane things like household bills. But she wouldn't stop badgering him. Every evening when Seth came home from the office, Carol was waiting to ask him why he hadn't checked on Cory, or why he chose his work over his family. She knew that it wouldn't do any good, but it didn't matter. She usually pounced before he could set down his bag. "How could you choose your fucking computer over your son?"

"I've told you, I made a mistake. I've admitted it a million times. Jesus, I have to live with it now, you know."

"Why'd you even get married and have a child if you were going to be so selfish?"

"You've always gotten what you wanted, haven't you?"

"Not your time. I do everything around here. You've always been married to your work, not me."

Seth shook his head. "I should have known better than to leave him in your hands. You're only on Seth time."

He stared at her and blinked a couple of times.

"My baby's dead because of you!" she yelled, her face looking fierce as her voice cracked.

"Cory was my child too."

"He was more mine, and you know it! I did everything for him. Being a good bread winner doesn't make you a father, Seth."

"Go to hell."

Carol would slam a cupboard or a door and retreat to the guest room with a pint of vanilla Häagen-Dazs. They agreed to go to therapy—together and separately. The fights were replaced by silence. Carol hardly ate anything but ice cream. It soothed her. Every night she dove into her vanilla, and every morning she hated Seth more and felt guilty about taking the call from her agent. Seth stayed out late, some nights not returning home at all. Six months later he moved into an apartment.

Brigitte visited Carol twice a month. After Cory's death, Carol had closed the door to his room. She wouldn't go near it. But she knew that his room was fully intact. She pictured his Legos still scattered all over the carpet in there. She felt like she was being held under water and was only allowed to take an occasional small breath. One Saturday she planned to be out of the house. She had Brigitte box up and take Cory's toys, clothes, and shoes to St. Vincent's. Another Saturday she had Brigitte arrange workers to haul off Cory's furniture. Brigitte painted the apple green walls a smooth cream color. She helped Carol choose new colors and furniture for the rest of the house, listened to her complain about Seth, walked with her along the Marina, held her when she cried. Seth filed for divorce. Carol told her lawyer she wanted to strip him naked. He didn't put up a fight. She got the house and three quarters of their investment portfolio.

The rain lightens to sprinkles. People walk by without umbrellas. Brigitte checks her phone for messages. She walks to the curb and looks up and down the sidewalk. A school bus passes Brigitte, and she waves at some kids in the back. Carol stares at Brigitte's baby. Brigitte will hand her the baby, she knows she will. Her stomach turns. She'd spent hours running her hand over Cory's skin, smelling him, watching him sleep—his little eyebrows bunch up and smooth out, his lips purse and relax, his chest rise and fall. She'd whisper, "My sweet baby." She used to look at him like Brigitte looks at her baby. She wipes her eyes and blows her nose. In a recent meditation class she has learned to focus on her breath. She tries to do this now, but it doesn't work. She watches Brigitte. She's always been the perfect friend. That's the problem. She never puts Carol in her place when she's being bitchy or cruel. She always supports Carol, always does whatever Carol wants. Carol looks at her friend waiting for her, a concerned look on Brigette's face, and she says, "You're pathetic." She opens the passenger door, sets the ice cream on the curb, and closes the door.

Brigitte paces along the sidewalk and pulls out her phone. Carol's phone rings. She tosses it in the glove box, grabs the steering wheel, and looks at the side mirror. A line of cars is coming. She focuses on her breath. Her face becomes serious, even stern. I can do this. The cars are passing by. Her phone rings. I have to do this. She thinks of Seth sitting on that couch with his head in his laptop. Thinks of her agent calling her at the wrong time. Thinks of that house whose hallway was too long to hear anything. She thinks of Brigitte smiling proudly and handing her the baby. She looks into the side mirror. The last car in the line approaches. Carol starts the car and grips the wheel. Brigitte turns toward the café and talks into the phone. The street is clear. Carol pulls out and drives away without looking back at Brigitte and her baby. She does not know where she is going. She passes under a row of sycamore trees but only sees Cory's hair floating softly like grass in still water.

# THE SHORT REIGN OF CHEF GERARD

The afternoon a white truck came to Mukoko, Chef Gerard had been the *chef du village* only a month. This was his chance to show the villagers that he could be in charge, as his father had been for 21 years. As he did most days, he sat under an avocado tree in front of his mud hut drinking palm wine. His dusty old t-shirt and shorts smelled of dirt, sweat, and alcohol. Thick yellow toenails jutted up from his knobby feet. Between swigs he stroked his soft mustache. He thought of his first month as *chef* and fumed. When he became *chef* after his father died, the village didn't honor him with a *fete*. Nobody brought him a calabash of palm wine, or a cluster of bananas, or even came to shake his hand. His wife cooked a chicken, but that happened once a month anyway. The worst was that even after a month, nobody called him *chef*. He thought it was because at 38 he had the body of a pubescent boy. He spotted the truck stirring up savannah dust on the only road that led to the village, and he smiled.

Chef Gerard kicked a pecking chicken as he walked into the middle of the road and stopped the truck. It was the same two

Swedish missionaries—a man and woman—that had always donated bags of clothes to the village. They all shook hands.

"You can leave the clothes here," Chef Gerard told them.

"But the old *chef* always had us drop them at the church."

"The old *chef* is dead. I'm in charge now. I'll make sure the people get the clothes."

The *chef's* wife and twelve-year-old son approached carrying buckets of water on their heads. Sweat rolled down their cheeks, and they were winded from walking up from the small river.

"This is no time for water," Chef Gerard said. "Help them with these clothes."

Mama Boma set down her bucket and scurried toward the truck. But Tiko sat down and drank some water. The *chef* walked over to him. "Good work, son. When you finish, come help."

Twenty villagers gathered near the truck, and dozens more wove around mud huts toward the *chef's* home. When they had seen the truck, *mamas* stopped hoeing, *tatas* stopped drinking, and children stopped playing. Those outside of Mukoko heard others yelling about the clothes, and they came running.

One *tata* asked his wife, "They seem early this year, no?"

"*Eh.* This is good. I need some new blouses."

Children skipped and asked if they'd get a shirt or some pants or even a dress. The parents just said, "*Hurry up.*"

From the truck bed, the Swedish man said, "*Chef,* if we go to the church, more people will be able to—"

"No. I will handle the clothes from here."

The Swedes looked at each other and raised their eyebrows. They moved the big black bags to the tailgate.

The crowd grew large. Some said, "Why are they doing it here? This isn't the way we do it."

Chef Gerard told his wife and son to move the bags into their hut. They carried away a bag apiece.

"Hey Gerard, when are we going to get our clothes?" Tata Katanga asked.

The *chef* didn't respond. He just watched his wife and son grab more bags.

Tata Katanga's wife elbowed him. "You fool, call him *chef.*"

Tata Katanga made a face at her and shook his head.
The wife and boy returned for more bags. Just one was left. Tata
Katanga said, "Our dear *chef*, when are we going to get our clothes?"
The *chef* picked up the last bag himself. "We want to sort them
first." He went inside and closed the door.

One hundred villagers waved goodbye to the Swedes and
watched their truck disappear into the savannah. Then they turned
and watched the door of the hut. "What is he doing? We should all
be at the church," Tata Katanga said. *Tatas* and some *mamas* nodded
and said, "*Eh.*" Children asked where their clothes were.

The door crept open. The *chef* pranced out wearing an
oversized navy blue blazer. He'd once been to Kikwit and had seen
the businessmen downtown in their suits, looking so proud and
important. The crowd grew silent. Most gawked. The big blazer
made Chef Gerard look even smaller, but he strutted around on the
hardpan dirt looking at the others looking at him. He walked back
and forth, and the villagers stood with their mouths agape. They
looked at their own threadbare clothes and looked back at the *chef*,
their eyes glued to the blue blazer. They watched him fiddle with
the blazer's inside pockets as if he had a wallet, business cards, or
handkerchief. He held one side of the blazer open and ran his hand
down the satin lining. He looked at the label and read it aloud to
himself. He folded a piece of paper into a triangle and placed it in
the breast pocket and then buttoned the blazer. Then he flipped up
his collar and jammed his hands in the blazer's front pockets.

"What about *our* clothes, *chef*?" Tata Katanga asked.

Chef Gerard didn't look at him. He stroked his mustache a
couple times. "Come tomorrow." He walked back inside and closed
the door.

"That bastard."

"Shhh, you," Tata Katanga's wife said.

"But he's playing with us."

"Don't be stupid, you."

Others shook their heads.

"He thinks he can do what he wants now that he's the *chef du
village*. If his cousin were not the head of the tribunal I'd—"

"Shhh, you, or you'll get fined."

*

Most villagers skipped their *fufu* breakfast and hurried to claim some clothes at sunrise. The *chef* had sorted the clothing into three piles—men's, women's, and children's.

"Look at all the pants this year," a *tata* said. "And shirts with buttons."

"And the skirts."

"I hope there are more blazers."

"Where's mine?" children asked. Parents pointed, and the children smiled.

The villagers spread out along the edge of the parcel like runners lining up to race.

The *chef* emerged wearing the blazer and eating his breakfast. He pulled wads from a ball of *fufu*, chewed open-mouthed, and smacked his lips. He stood against the hut looking out over the people at the savannah.

The crowd quietly watched. Nobody disturbed the *chef's* meal until the elder Tata Dabu asked, "Hey *chef*, can we get some clothes and leave so you can eat in peace?"

The *chef* didn't respond. He took his last bite, set down the bowl, and walked to the edge of his lot. Everybody crouched, ready to sprint to the clothes. Chef Gerard looked at everybody. "This year the clothes are for sale."

All the people, from the gray to the toddling, stood up straight. Children looked at their parents, and parents looked at the *chef*, who fingered his blazer's buttons.

Old Tata Dabu asked, "Why are you selling the clothes, *chef*? Your father and your grandfather always gave them away."

"I'm the *chef* now, and that's how it's going to be. If you can't pay with money, then I will accept palm wine, chickens, fish, peanuts, bananas, salt, sugar, plantains, bows, arrows, spears, machetes, and even manioc flour."

Before the *chef* had finished his list, most of the people had shaken their heads and walked away, many pulling children who screamed. "I want my shirt! I want my pants!"

A few stayed and rummaged through the clothes, but nobody

bought anything. Only Tata Katanga remained, stroking his patchy beard.

"Chef Gerard, you are smart for trying to make some money, very smart. But we've known each other a long time."

Chef Gerard looked at him blankly.

"We grew up together, so maybe you can let me *have* a new shirt? Look, mine has holes."

The *chef* turned and walked away.

"You bastard," Tata Katanga said under his breath.

*

The *chef* made his son, Tiko, change clothes throughout the day. At any given time, villagers saw the boy in shorts or pants, in a t-shirt or a button-down, in a sweater or a vest. No other kid in Mukoko had more than two shirts, let alone different pairs of shorts. Every father heard the same question from their children: "Why can't *I* have clothes like Tiko?"

Chef Gerard also made Mama Boma change her clothes two or three times a day. In the morning, Mama Boma wore a dress to pound manioc. At noon she'd change into a skirt and blouse to haul water. In the late afternoon she'd put on a sarong, t-shirt, and floppy hat to sweep the lot. The other women noticed all of this and let their husbands know about it. "Look at her. Don't you want me to look that nice?"

The men didn't respond to their children or wives, nor did they share that they had paid the *chef* a visit.

"Chef Gerard, your father and I were good friends, and I knew your grandfather," Tata Dabu said.

"Our mothers were close," another said.

"Remember the time you and I went hunting together?" another said.

They all tried, but the *chef* turned and walked away from all of them.

One night, as a full moon rose, the men met outside the village, where the savannah grass was high.

"Let's just wait until it's late and then take the clothes that should have been ours from the beginning," Tata Katanga said.

"He might see."

"He won't if it's late enough," Tata Katanga said smiling.
The other men shook their heads. "It's too risky."

Tata Katanga waited until 2:00 a.m. He tiptoed to Chef Gerard's property. It was quiet. Chef Gerard's chickens and goats were asleep up against the hut. He heard someone snoring inside. Tata Katanga dropped down on all fours, crawled toward the children's pile and grabbed a pair of jeans for his son. As he turned around, he hit his head on Chef Gerard's shins.

Chef Gerard looked down at Tata Katanga.

"I'm sorry, my dear *chef*. I must have had too much palm wine. I didn't mean to do this." He folded the jeans and set them on the pile. "I'm so sorry, my dear *chef*." Chef Gerard walked inside his hut.

The next day a sharp rap on the door awoke Tata Katanga. He opened the door to see the *chef* and the head of the tribunal, a round man wearing a tweed blazer that Chef Gerard had given him.

"Is this him?" the head of the tribunal asked.

"Yes," Chef Gerard said.

The head of the tribunal nodded at Chef Gerard and faced Tata Katanga. "I am the head of the tribunal. For attempting to steal, you will pay the honorable *chef* two goats, or you will come with me to Lamba to spend a month in jail. Which do you choose?"

Tata Katanga's wife edged alongside him. "You stole?"

"Not exactly."

She slapped his shoulder. "You! What were you thinking? Now we won't eat meat for a year!"

Tata Katanga flinched.

Chef Gerard and the head of the tribunal looked at each other and smiled.

Tata Katanga tethered two goats resting in the shade alongside their hut and handed the *chef* the end of a rope. Tata Katanga watched the two men walk away, the two goats bouncing along as if nothing were wrong.

Before leaving Mukoko, the higher official shared a meal with the *chef's* family. "I always enjoy coming here because I can see my favorite sister and my favorite cousin in one trip." When he left he said, "Let me know if you need any more help, Gerard."

*

Chickens started to nest in the mounds of clothes and goats nibbled away at them. Mama Boma asked the *chef,* "Why don't you give away those clothes?"

"You got new blouses and dresses and the boy got new clothes, so why do you care?"

"They're going to waste, Gerard."

"So what."

The mounds of clothes became piles of shredded fabric, loose buttons, and odd rivets that the goats and chickens slept on.

\*

Chef Gerard needed to address the community, so he went to church on Sunday. The tall priest did a double-take when he saw him enter the open-air church. He waved him up to the front. The *chef* strutted past dozens of onlookers.

"Whoa, can you believe it?" one *mama* asked another.

"First time since he was a boy."

"His mama would be proud."

The adults didn't shift, the children didn't fidget, the babies didn't cry.

The *chef* strutted up to the pulpit. "I enjoy very good palm wine, and I make the best in Mukoko. Unfortunately, some of the trees on my lot do not produce as much juice as I need, so I will have to use some of your trees."

The women looked at the men, whose eyes bulged.

Tata Katanga said to himself, "What's he doing now, that—"

"Shh, you."

"Tomorrow I will mark the trees that I will take control of."

Tata Katanga stood. "Please *chef*—" but Chef Gerard walked right down the center aisle past him and out of the church.

The priest said, "May God help us."

Old, middle-aged, and young men gathered outside the church.

"He's threatening our lives."

"It has taken me years to perfect my palm wine."

"My wine is who I am."

"What will I do if he takes my trees?"

"You'll be like a woman," said Tata Dabu, silencing the group.

None of the men slept that night.

The next day, each man waited just beyond the *chef's* lot to see whose trees he would usurp. The *chef* came out with long strips of torn t-shirts stuffed in his blazer pockets and headed straight for the river. The men turned to each other. "He's going to Tata Katanga's!" Tata Katanga grew pale.

There, the *chef* walked to the far side of the lot, where the ground was very soft, and tied a strip of material around a fat palm towering overhead. Tata Katanga dropped to his knees. "Please, *chef*, not *that* tree! Have all the others if you want, but not *that* tree." Chef Gerard walked away and continued on to six other lots, where six other men begged and offered to wash his clothes or fetch his water or give him half of their palm wine. Each time the *chef* said nothing and walked away.

\*

The *chef* visited the trees weekly. He would snicker to himself if any of the men watched him shin up his tree, pop off the calabash, and throw back a smooth refreshing splash of palm wine. He'd lean back in his woven harness and lick his lips. "Mmmm, *mbote mingi*." The onlooker would tighten his fists or clench his teeth or curse the *chef* under his breath and wave off his wife who'd say something about being fined. The victim would become even more furious when he would run out of his own palm wine and was then forced to pay the *chef* for wine from his own tree. If the *chef* saw others near the trees, he'd make an official visit, even if he'd been there the day before. By noon, Chef Gerard would carry home two calabashes of palm wine. He usually drank one and sold the other.

\*

Mama Boma routinely hoed her manioc field with another large woman, Mama Adoma. One morning, while hoeing the sandy soil, Mama Adoma said, "Look at my old clothes."

Mama Boma glanced at her thin t-shirt and holey skirt and kept hoeing.

"Hey *mama*, why don't you give me some of your clothes?"

Mama Boma stopped and looked at her and then out at the savannah horizon. "I don't think my husband would let me."

Mama Adoma stood up straight and raised her eyebrows. "But we've been best friends since we were girls."

Mama Boma sighed.

That night at the dinner table, Tiko scooped cooked manioc leaves with wads of *fufu*, Chef Gerard drank from a calabash, and Mama Boma picked at her food. The sun had set, and their hut was growing dark. She lit the candle in the middle of the table. It began to flicker.

"Why aren't you eating?"

"I'm not hungry."

Tiko started to make figures out of his *fufu*.

"Stop that," Mama Boma said. "Don't yell at my boy."

She looked down.

The boy ran out to chase lightning bugs sparking the night-time air. Mama Boma looked at the *chef*.

"Today in the field Mama Adoma told me how nice I looked."

The *chef* looked at her and stroked his mustache.

"I like all my clothes, Gerard, but I have so many. So I'd like to give her a couple—"

"*Ve.*"

"But her shirt is so thin, Gerard, and—"

"*Ve,*" he said, raising his voice.

"But Gerard, she's my friend, and—"

His chair fell behind him as he shot up and slapped her across the mouth. "*Ve, ve, ve!* Can't you understand me, you cow?"

"Why not?" she cried.

"If she wanted a shirt, she should have bought one."

Mama Boma buried her face in her hands.

"Go ahead and cry, you spoiled baby." He grabbed a calabash and disappeared into sparkled darkness.

*

With a swollen lip, Mama Boma met Mama Adoma at the river. "I'm sorry, but I can't give away any of my clothes."

"Hmph." Mama Adoma placed her bucket atop her head and walked away.

When Mama Boma tried to talk to Mama Adoma in the field or after church, or if they met up on a narrow path, Mama Adoma looked away.

The other women in the village also shunned Mama Boma.
They didn't greet her, never dropped off mangoes or papayas, didn't
even walk by her hut. She couldn't give away any of her clothes, but she didn't have
to stand out. She'd wear her old clothes. The other women would
then see that she was one of them. She rummaged through all her
clothes in her dresser but didn't find a stitch of old clothing. So
she rummaged through them again. Then she went outside. The *chef*
was sitting on the ground drinking palm wine and rubbing the satin
lining of his blazer.

"Have you seen my old clothes?" she asked.

He waited awhile before looking up at her. "I don't want you to
look dirty, like all the other *mamas*."

"I want my clothes."

He took a swig of palm wine and looked at her. "I burned
them."

She bit her lower lip and went inside, slamming the door behind
her.

*

For weeks some children had been following Tiko around.
In the morning when they first saw him, they would examine his
Hawaiian shirt or wool pants or red corduroy overalls or whatever
he wore. They'd tuck in their shirts if Tiko's was tucked in. If it was
out, they'd leave theirs out. Kids pulled Tiko aside to ask for some
clothes.

"Just give me what you don't want anymore."

"*Ve.*"

"A t–shirt?"

"*Ve.*"

"One of your dirty shirts?"

Always "*Ve*," and always the kids still stuck close to Tiko.

The rainy season began. One afternoon after the daily
downpour, Tiko led eight followers down the steep bank just past
Tata Katanga's house to the small river. Downstream Tata Katanga
and Digu, his teenage son, stood in the river with raised spears. They
stared into the water. The rains had given patches of the soft soil on
the banks a quicksand effect. Tiko walked right into a moist patch.

His eyes widened. "Oh God, I'm sinking!" He waved his arms, looking terrified. The boys froze. Tiko sank to his calves and then to his knees. The boys yelled, "Help! Help!" A second later Tiko laughed, pulled up his legs, and walked out of the muck. The other boys laughed and started playing in the soft soil, imitating Tiko. Tata Katanga and Digu came running along the river holding spears with fish on them.

"What's wrong?" Tata Katanga asked.

"Nothing. We're only playing," Tiko said.

Tata Katanga walked away, but Digu stayed.

"Hey, Tiko, why'd your dad marry his cousin?"

Tiko said nothing.

"Your mom and dad are cousins?"one boy asked.

Tiko turned red. "No. They're not."

"Yes they are. *They're cousins*," Digu said. "That's gross."

Tiko looked away.

Digu stared at Tiko. "You and all your fancy clothes. You think you're a *chef* just like your dad, don't you?"

Tiko turned to his followers. "Let's go."

They didn't move. Tiko glanced at the big teenager.

"Too scared to talk, Tata Clothes?"

Tiko turned to walk away, but Digu grabbed his arm, whipped him around, and let go, sending him into the mud on his back. He started to cry.

"Waaa waaaa baby Tata Clothes," Digu said and laughed. "Waaa waaa baby Tata Clothes."

The other boys stared at Tiko. He stood up and tried to run at Digu, but he slipped and fell on his face. Digu pointed and laughed harder, and the other boys laughed too.

Tiko got up and started to run away, but Digu grabbed the back of his shorts and ripped them, exposing Tiko's bare butt.

"Look at baby Tata Clothes now!" Digu said.

The boys howled with laughter. Tiko ran up the bank trying to cover his backside with the flapping fabric, the boys' laughter slapping him the whole time.

Tiko cried all the way home. He stepped over his father sleeping in the shade, as did Mama Boma minutes later, when she returned home with long sticks of firewood on her head. Villagers had heard Tiko and came to the edge of the *chef's* bare parcel. Mama Boma dropped her load on the ground and rushed into the house. The shutters were closed, so it took a second for her to see him sitting on his wooden bed sobbing.

She ran to him. "You're all dirty. What happened?"

"He called me baby Tata Clothes, and the boys laughed at me."

"Huh?"

"Digu. He threw me in the mud, and all the boys laughed at me."

"Why did he do *that?*"

"Because of my clothes."

Mama Boma pulled her son into her big bosom and hugged him. He sobbed. She thought of Mama Adoma and the other women who no longer talked with her. She thought of her husband hitting her. She thought of him burning her clothes. She held her crying boy and clenched her jaw and looked toward the door.

She heard the *chef* out front. "Damn that fat cow. She woke me up."

Mama Boma let go of Tiko and marched outside. People had gathered and were listening to the *chef* complain about her. She grabbed the *chef's* arm and pulled him up off the ground. "Do you know what you've done?"

Chef Gerard jerked his arm away, brushed off his sleeve, and looked at her bug eyed.

"You've ruined me and Tiko."

The *chef* turned. More villagers were coming.

"Don't talk to me like that, woman!"

She got in his face. "Don't tell me what to do."

"Oh!" the crowd said.

He pointed at the door. "Get in there!"

Mama Boma turned and headed into the hut, her heels thumping the ground like a drum.

The *chef* turned to the crowd. "Pardon, but I need to teach my wife a lesson." He opened the door and stepped inside.

Before his eyes could adjust, Mama Boma hit him over the head with a pot. "Oh, my head!" Tiko sat and watched. The *chef* darted to the other side of the table, panting and shaking. Mama Boma grabbed a chair and hurled it at him, but he deflected it. She lunged over the table, clutched his blazer collar, and yanked his head into the table. Blood ran down his face. "Ahhhh!" he screamed. He tried to run, but she got him in a headlock and squeezed tight. She dragged him to the door and threw him out. He hit the dirt with an "Ugh."

The crowd gasped. The men looked at each other and smiled.

Chef Gerard jumped up. He had a gash above his eyebrow and his forehead was swelling. He wiped blood from his nose and mouth with his sleeve. The blazer was torn under the arms and covered with dust. He looked at it like a child does a broken toy. He brushed himself off and turned toward the door. "I'm not finished with her."

The crowd laughed. Chef Gerard jerked around and they went silent.

He strutted back into the hut. Mama Boma hit him over the head with the same pot, dropping him to his knees. She kicked him in the face with her heel, and he fell onto his back. She picked him up like a wet rag, carried him to the door, and threw him higher and farther. He hit the ground with a louder thud.

"Oh!" the crowd said, holding their hands over their mouths to avoid laughing. The *chef* lay still for a while, groaning. He slowly sat up and rubbed his head. The crowd watched and whispered. The *chef* brushed off his blazer and looked up at the others. "I need to let her heal. She's hurting real bad."

Mama Boma flung open the door and carried out armfuls of clothes—women's, men's, children's. She threw them into the crowd. "Here, take these, take whatever you want. Take them all."

The villagers pounced on them, smiling and laughing.

Chef Gerard stood. "What are you doing, woman?"

Mama Boma moved toward him, and he flinched. She made multiple trips with armfuls of clothes and threw them into the crowd until they were all gone. "*Merci, mama,*" villagers said as they left. She went back inside and closed the door.

Chef Gerard picked up a calabash. It was empty. He found his harness on the side of the hut and limped off toward the river.

Crossing Tata Katanga's lot, the *chef* heard the family inside talking about the fight. "She threw him out the door like a sack of manioc!" They all laughed.

The *chef* slopped through the muck, affixed his harness around the fat palm, and shinned up it.

He plucked the calabash from the tree and took a couple of pulls. "Mmmm, *Mbote mingi.*" As he leaned back and went for a third, his harness broke. He fell head first, entering the soft soil up to his waist. Only his lower torso and two knobby legs jutted up from the earth. The bottom part of the blazer circled his inverted trunk like a skirt. His partially-bent legs were spread-eagle and didn't move. His thick, yellow toenails topped the whole sight.

From his hut, Tata Katanga had seen him fall. "Serves him right." He wanted to grab the full calabash also lodged in the soft soil, but he knew better than to go near the body. Tata Katanga sent Digu to tell the other villagers.

Everyone went down to the river to see the body, but nobody got too close. Not even Mama Boma and Tiko went near the stiff corpse. To do so would be to claim responsibility. So they left it.

# THROWN OUT IN THESSALONIKI

I had expected Thessaloniki to have some of the Greek charm I'd seen in movies—whitewashed buildings, cobblestone streets, sapphire-blue sea. None of it was there. The seaside was gray and smelled like sewage. Boring concrete buildings filled city blocks, old buses blew black exhaust, and drivers in lines of cars yelled and shot hand gestures at pesky scooters weaving through them. I was to live in an apartment on a narrow street lined with the same dull buildings.

After college, I'd gotten a marketing job with Citibank. Six months later I landed a one-year transfer to the Citibank in Thessaloniki. I wanted to get in touch with my Greek roots. My *mamá* had said, "You should contact my step-cousin, Vasili. Maybe he'll help you find a place. After all my father—your *papou*—did for him, he better."

I wrote Vasili. Two weeks later I received a postcard that read, "We're very excited to meet you. We have an apartment for you to live in. Let us know when you will arrive. Love, Vasili and Victoria." I was set.

When I got to Athens, I called Vasili. He gave me the address to the apartment in Thessaloniki, and we set a date. Vasili's comb-over didn't hide his baldness. He said, "Hello, boy," and hugged me lightly. He wore a gray suit and stood up straight, like he was trying to look as tall as Victoria. She shook my hand. She was coiffed--soft hair, manicured nails, a touch of make-up, a dark blue blazer with a monograph. She had Mona Lisa's mouth and Dracula's eyes. They were probably in their late forties. Victoria went to the kitchen, leaned against the wall, and looked out a small window. Vasili showed me the place. The big apartment was empty except for a table and two chairs in the kitchen and a twin-size bed, desk, and chair in a bedroom. The entry, kitchen, and bathrooms had marble floors; the bedrooms and living room hardwood. Many windows afforded a view of the city. Vasili and I stood out on the balcony that wrapped around the entire place. "Victoria grew up here. Her father's family owned this land. They built this building and the apartment building across the street."

It looked just like this one.

"Victoria's aunt still lives in one of the apartments. Victoria inherited this one when her father died. We rent the two other apartments. This one became vacant after you wrote. We held it for you."

"Why don't you live here?" I asked.

Vasili looked at me smugly. "We live in a place on the water. We'll have to have you to lunch."

"Thank you for making my move so easy."

Vasili pinched my cheek and said, "Let's go back into the kitchen to talk."

Victoria was still at the window. She folded her arms and looked out. Vasili and I sat down at the table. He leaned forward. "My father died when I was three and didn't leave my mother and me any money. He liked to play cards." He shook his head in disapproval. "My mother got a job as a maid, but it didn't pay much. We ate bread and beans in the summer when she had more work; in the winter there wasn't much work, so we mainly ate bread. Can you imagine, not being able to afford *beans*? I got one pair of shoes a year." His voice dropped. "When they had holes, I stuffed them with cardboard I pulled from trash bins. I wore the same clothes every day. Some months we couldn't pay the rent. The landlord was an old friend of my father's, so he didn't kick us out. I was sick often." He paused. "Then my aunt married your *papou*." Vasili's voice perked up. "Things changed because he started to send us $150 a month. That was a lot of money in the late 50's. We were able to buy some meat and always pay the rent. His money allowed me to study, not work, in high school. I passed the university entrance exam and became an accountant," he said proudly. "All this because of the money your *papou* sent us." He leaned forward and touched my shoulder. "While you are living here, you will not pay us." Victoria looked at us then out the window.

"Thank you," I said. "This is very generous."

"It's nothing compared to what your *papou* did for us."

They left, Victoria still not having said a word. I wondered why she had been cold. I went back out to the balcony. It was my first time abroad. I'd be making it on my own at 23 without my parents' help. I had my own *flat*; no more dorms.

*

I started at the bank the next day. It was on Tsimiski, a wide tree-lined street downtown with classy shops. I was to work with the marketing team in overhauling their ads. My desk was near the window. A quaint bookstore—Plato's Corner—sat across the street. After work that first day, I went there to buy a *Herald Tribune*. Next to the newspaper rack a woman in black sat with her legs crossed. She was a looker. Her brown eyes were big, like a model's. She moved her long, dark hair from one side to the other. She had to be around 30. I looked at the newspapers, then at her. She looked up at me, and I looked back at the papers. I grabbed a *Herald Tribune*.

"That's a good paper," the woman said.

"Excuse me?" I said, smiling.

"It's a *New York Times* paper. It's not scared to expose the ugly truth about Reagan."

"So you know newspapers?"

"I have to; this is my store. I must know what's on the shelves."

Despina and I talked for an hour—about politics, about Thessaloniki, about her, about me, about going out for a drink.

We went to a hip sidewalk bar on the water called Dionysis. She drank cognac; I had a beer. She had studied political science at university and had worked at Plato's Corner for eight years before the owner sold it to her. Per Greek custom, she lived at home because she wasn't married. She despised American imperialism. "At least the bank you work for is based in Europe," she told me. Drinks led to dinner and retsina wine at a nearby *taverna*. Different parties crowded around the eight wooden tables covered with lamb, *angouri-domata salata, spanikopita, patates, kalimaria*. The Greek music and chatter made it hard to hear. Despina moved her chair next to mine. By midnight we were smashed. We laughed at my accent and her habit of moving her hair from one side to the other. Each time we laughed, she put her hand on my knee, and I leaned into her. At 2:00 a.m. I put her in a cab, paid the driver, and walked home along the seaside looking at the beautifully lit buildings' reflections in the glassy sea.

This turned into a routine, me going into Despina's store after work and us going out. After a week of it, I suggested that we make dinner at my place before catching a movie. We didn't make dinner, but we made love in the kitchen and then smoked cigarettes in my twin bed. I wasn't a smoker, but it felt right with Despina. We walked to a neighborhood *souvlaki* stand holding hands. I felt awesome. The entire scene—an older European lover, the foreign tongue, the *souvlaki* cooking above coals—made me feel international and mature.

Despina and I started to rendezvous at my place on a regular basis. After the sex we'd smoke cigarettes like we were in the movies and lounge around naked in my apartment. Sometimes we met up with her friends for a late meal and hours of drinking retsina and smoking cigarettes in small, smoke-filled *tavernas*. Her friends were older, like her. I could tell that they thought I was young. They always wanted to talk politics. I got bored sometimes, but they included me in their discussion and liked when I poured myself more retsina and smoked more of their cigarettes. I felt like they saw me as a friend.

*

One day I was about to hand wash some clothes when the phone rang. It was Victoria.

"I understand that you've been bringing a girl to my house."

"Well, uh, I've met a very nice woman. She owns a business."

"We don't do that here."

"I'm twenty-three years old."

"That's right, you're still a child."

I did not respond.

"If this continues, I will have Vasili call your mother."

I nearly laughed. Then I pictured my *mamá* pulling the receiver in close, her lips pursing, her eyes squinting from humiliation, and suddenly it wasn't very funny.

"Understood," I said.

"Good. And no smoking either," she said and hung up.

I stared at the phone. Who would have told her? The two guys above me were dental students buried in books. And the old woman on the bottom floor liked me because I swept the walkway. Then it hit me—her aunt. I pictured this old *yia yia* with nothing better to do but spy on the American and report everything she saw to her niece and spread gossip. A peeping aunt. What a nightmare.

*

Despina and I had to change our habits. She wasn't happy about it. "How are we supposed to be a couple if we can't have sex? You should move out."

It was a good idea, but I feared Vasili reporting that I'd not appreciated their offer. I could explain everything to my *mamá*. She'd see Victoria's irrationality, but she would also say, "Why'd you go over there and start trouble? Especially with *those* people?" I couldn't let down my *mamá*.

When I was growing up, my *papou* and step-*yia yia*—grandfather and step-grandmother—lived down the street. I never met my real *yia yia*; she had died when my *mamá* was thirteen. My *mamá* didn't like her step-*mamá* because she criticized her average grades, chubby body, and crooked teeth. When my *mamá* went to business college in Hayward, she had to live in the basement of a boarding house, mice scampering over her as she slept. My *papou* couldn't afford anything better because of the $150 he sent to Greece every month. My *mamá* resented Vasili and his mother. Even after my step-*yia yia* and my *papou* died, my *mamá* didn't forgive them for neglecting her.

"I can't move out right now," I told Despina. "Maybe in a few months after things smooth out."

"A few *months*? God, that means we'll have to go to the Hercules."

It was a cheap hotel that charged by the hour. It was off one of the main streets. The walls, bed spread, and sheets were riddled with cigarette burns. After the first time I didn't want to go back, but I didn't want to disappoint Despina any more.

I splurged on a phone call to the States. I didn't tell my *mamá* about the Victoria incident. My *mamá* said, "So Vasili came through. Good, he owed me." She told me to call my relatives in Pinakates. "It's three hours away. They live in the same stone house your *papou* was born in. Call them, okay?"

"Okay."

"Don't just say 'Okay.' Call them; it's important that you meet our blood. You must go to the village to see where you're from. Will you call them?"

"Yes, I'll call them, *mamá*."

Not feeling any great need, I waited a few weeks before calling them one holiday weekend. I'd never met my second cousin, but Effie was overjoyed to hear that I was in Greece. When I told her where I lived, she said, "*Thessaloniki!* Mary is studying at the university there. I live with her during the school year. We're only in the village this weekend for the holiday." I told her my address. "That's five blocks from us!" she said. "When we get back to Thessaloniki, you'll have to come over for lunch."

I looked forward to the lunch, but I'd have to keep my social life to myself. Effie was old school, definitely not the type to understand.

*

Despina and I were walking down Tsimiski when a man weaving around cars on an old Vespa caught my eye. He was so sure of himself, sitting upright, gliding through the traffic and looking regal in a Fidel Castro way, with a goatee and army-green jacket. Despina yelled, "Daviko!" When he spotted her, he squeezed between two parked cars and pulled up on the sidewalk, smiling the whole way. He spoke fast and with an alluring passion.

They kissed on both cheeks. "Where have you been, darling?"

"Working at the store and showing George around Thessaloniki."

His smile fell. "Who?"

Despina turned toward me. "This is George."

"Nice to meet you," I said, extending my hand.

He shook my hand fast and studied me. "You speak with an accent."

"I'm from *Ameriki*."

He slowly nodded. "What are you doing in Greece?"

"I'm here for a year, working at the Citibank across from Despina's store."

"You work at a *bank*?"

I nodded, trying to figure out this guy's problem.

"So I presume you've studied at university. What subject?"

"Marketing."

He tilted his head and looked at me without blinking.

Despina moved her hair to one side. "George studied at Berkeley," she said. Daviko's face lit up.

"Ah, where the students protested in the 60's. Excellent movement. Their leader was very good at standing up to the capitalist swine."

I pictured Berkeley legend Mario Savio atop a trapped police car rallying thousands of protesting students.

"Where did you learn your Greek?"

"My parents are Greek."

"Ah, so you're *Greek*."

"Well, Greek-American," I said, bobbing my head.

He looked at me and didn't say anything. The pause became uncomfortable.

"I must go," he abruptly said. He leaned in close to my ear and said, "Georgie, remember that your blood is Greek."

I didn't know how to respond, so I didn't.

He kick-started his Vespa. He whispered something into Despina's ear, kissed her, and slid into the traffic. Despina watched him ride for a block. I wondered why she had never mentioned him.

"What did he say to you?" she asked.

"For me to remember that my blood is Greek. What did he say to you?"

"He asked why I was with an American."

∗

I was listening to the Voice of America sports report on my radio when Mary came to invite me to Sunday lunch. I opened the door. Mary smiled big with crooked teeth and wide eyes before kissing me on both cheeks. She wore a plain, crocheted sweater, faded jeans, and scuffed sneakers. She stared at me like a long-lost brother.

"We're so happy that you're here," she said.

I couldn't believe how nice she was. I only wished that Effie were with her. Now peeping aunt would have something to report to Victoria even though Despina hadn't been back to the apartment.

Effie and Mary lived in the dark bottom unit of a brick apartment building that smelled of mold. Effie greeted me at the door with smiles and kisses. She wore all black. A stroke had killed her husband two years before. There was a front room, kitchen, and one bedroom. Mary studied and slept in the bedroom; Effie cooked, crocheted, and slept in the kitchen. On the small table sat a picture of Effie with her three sisters—four women wearing black. A small, wood-burning stove was the only source of heat.

Effie had made bread, beans, salad, and *dolmathes*. The food was the best I'd had in Greece. I ate two plates of it, making myself and Effie very happy. I expected to be there 90 minutes tops; we were at that table four hours. They told me about the relatives farming olives and scraping by with little. Effie told me about my *papou's* visit in 1965. What a homecoming it was for the man who'd hopped on a boat for *Ameriki* 50 years before, when he was fourteen. "We ate goat the entire time he was here," she said. I couldn't believe how much I liked being there. The scene was like our table at home, where my parents constantly told my sister and me their stories—about when they met at church, about them nearly going broke in Santa Barbara, about them almost losing our family's corner store.

I looked at my watch. I had to meet Despina downtown. I told Effie and Mary that I had work to do. We agreed to spend our Sundays together. I walked away happy about our plan.

That night I met Despina at Dionysis. The black sea was choppy. I excitedly told her about my day. She said, "The mother chaperones the daughter? That's so village."

I'd never seen this side of her. A few weeks before she had enthusiastically showed me a book of photographic images of Greek villagers like Effie and Mary. "Isn't the simple village life beautiful?" she'd asked.

I didn't bring it up. I didn't want to make her madder, but I did say, "They are my relatives, you know."

"Oh, and you're so close to them. You didn't even know them before today."

She crossed her legs and turned her stone face to look out at the black water. We didn't say anything for many minutes. Our time together had started to become a little boring. We still talked politics and had sex at the Hercules, but even that had gotten old. When I tried to talk about home and share that I missed things like watching football with my friends, eating Mexican food, and speaking English, her eyes always glazed over. We had started to go to a lot of movies. When we were at cafés or bars, there were often long moments of silence. A waiter approached our table and asked if we wanted anything else. "No," Despina said without looking at him.

"Let's walk down Tsimiski and window shop," I suggested.

She didn't say anything, but she got up and grabbed her black leather jacket.

The stores were closed, but their windows were lit up. Despina loved shoes, so we spent time looking at shoe displays. Other couples strolled down Tsimiski. An occasional car or scooter passed by.

"Look at the blue suede ones with the rounded toe. Aren't they beautiful?"

"They're nice," I said, only caring that her mood was lightening. She took my hand.

Still looking at the display, she said, "The symphony is playing next weekend. We should go."

"Saturday night would be great."

"I have to record our inventory. We'll have to go to the Sunday matinee performance."

I dreaded what I was about to say. I took a deep breath and said, "I've agreed to have lunch with Effie and Mary on Sunday."

Despina pulled away her hand. "Again? What, is this going to be a weekly date?"

I nodded.

She turned away and folded her arms. "You don't even know them."

"Despina, they're my relatives."

"They're your *relatives*, they're your *relatives*. First we have to go to the Hercules because of some *relatives*, and now you're going to spend Sundays with your *other* relatives. What about *me?*"

A scooter honked and pulled up onto the sidewalk.

"Daviko!" Despina said and practically jumped on him to hug and kiss him. It didn't feel good to see. He planted one on her lips, as if I wasn't standing a meter away.

"What have you been up to, darling?" he asked, not looking at me.

Despina smiled. "You remember George, don't you?" she said and moved her hair to the other side of her face.

He gave me an upward nod and turned back to her. "You and your hair. You know you would look good with short hair, darling. You have the face for it."

She gleamed.

"Listen, I'm having a dinner party Friday. I want you to be there," he said.

"That sounds great. We'll be there."

At least she included me in her plans.

"Banks are open Friday night. Don't you have to work?" he asked me.

"Not my department. I get off early on Fridays." I almost grinned in his face.

He tilted his head and stared at me dead-faced. I stared back, loving every awkward second, watching his beady eyes try to burn a hole into me as his stubbly face turned red.

"Okay," Despina said, "what time should we arrive?"

"Six." He kick-started his Vespa. He leaned over and kissed Despina. "You're beautiful, darling," he said. He took off down the street. She watched him until he turned two blocks later.

"Why do you let him kiss you like that?"

"What, you Americans don't kiss when you greet each other?"

"You know what I mean. You just encourage that letch when you smile at him."

"Don't call Daviko a letch. He's my friend from long ago."

"Well he doesn't see you as a friend, and you seem to like it."

"Is somebody jealous?" she said with a small smile.

"I don't like how he treats me. And you play along with it."
She took hold of my hand. We started to walk. "Daviko is just
a friend."

*

Mary dropped by with a plate of Effie's *baklava*. Like before,
I wished that Effie had been with her so that peeping aunt would
see a different side of me. I fixed us some tea. We sat at the kitchen
table and talked and ate the fresh, flaky *baklava*. She wore the same
sweater, faded jeans, and scuffed tennis shoes. Everything was
"wonderful" to Mary—her studies of the classics, them living in a
city, me living nearby. Being around her positive energy made me feel
lighter. I thought Despina could learn something from her.

I walked her out, we kissed on both cheeks, and she said, "See
you Sunday."

I wasn't upstairs five minutes when the phone rang.

"I understand another girl is now coming to my house."

"Hi Victoria. Yes, another girl is coming here—my cousin from
Pinakates who is studying classics at the university and lives five
blocks away with her mother."

"Well it still doesn't look good. Her mother should be with her
when she visits you."

"Victoria, she's my cousin."

"And that is my house."

Neither of us spoke. "Understood," I finally said, again picturing
my *mamá* receiving a call from Vasili.

"Good," Victoria said and hung up.

I slammed down the phone and saw that the blinds were open.
Peeping aunt would probably tell Victoria that I'd gotten mad. I
pulled the blinds shut.

*

A huge Soviet flag covered a wall in Daviko's apartment. It hung
above a table with a small bust of Lenin and pictures of Stalin and
Mao. A banner above the flag read, "Communist Party of Greece."
All this commie stuff was no joke. It was the real thing. It scared me.
Daviko wore a tunic and watched me as I glanced at his altar. When
I turned toward him, he smiled like the rat he was.

Two other couples were there. We sat at a large black table

with Daviko at the head, next to Despina. He passed around boiled beef, carrots, and potatoes—Lenin and company approved of the proletariat menu. Daviko raised a glass and said, "To the movement." The others raised their glasses, but I didn't.

"So what do you think of Gorbachev's leadership abilities? Is he furthering the cause or sleeping with Reagan?" Daviko asked.

Despina laughed and smiled at Daviko. I hooked a foot around one of hers, but she didn't respond, so I moved mine back.

"Gorbachev is too soft. He's letting that pig Reagan push him around," a woman in a beret said.

"Hear, hear," a mustached man said, raising his glass.

"Let's hear from the American," Daviko said.

"What American?" the mustached man asked.

"This boy here is American," he said, pointing at me.

Boy! What a prick. The others stared at me.

"George, tell us what you think of your President Reagan," Daviko said.

I took a sip of wine and leaned back. "I think most of what he says is hollow, that his economic strategy is dangerous, and that the world will pay the price of his politics for many years to come."

"Bravo," a man wearing round glasses said as Daviko looked on. Despina squeezed my thigh. Forks and knives returned to plates.

"Won't it be nice when the Americans finally wake up from their capitalist sleep?" the woman in the beret said.

"Don't count on it happening; they're too stupid to wake up," Daviko replied, winking at Despina. She giggled.

I tried to keep my cool, but my forehead started to feel warm.

"Let's hear from the American boy again," Daviko said. "What do you think, Georgie, will you Americans ever wake up, or are you too stupid?"

I tried to ignore the jabs. I told myself to stay cool. I sipped more wine. They looked at me. "I think Americans will eventually see through Reagan and move to the left," I said.

All heads nodded.

"But I don't think they'll embrace communism."

"Oh? So you Americans *are* stupid," Daviko said.

I sipped my wine and leaned back. "Maybe to you, but Americans see images of stores in East Germany with nothing on the shelves, and Poles rallying for change, and cities in Eastern Block countries looking depressed and gray, and all they see is a system that has bankrupted millions of lives." Daviko leaned forward. "Don't you realize that that's American propaganda?" Despina looked at me nervously. The others stopped chewing and looked at me too. The pressure to agree with the host pushed on me. I wasn't going to do it. "The way the information is presented may be propagandistic, but nobody can deny the grim situations in these countries." Daviko stared at his wine glass and tilted his head. I wiped sweat from my forehead. Despina wouldn't look at me. "So tell me, George, your blood is Greek, and you speak Greek, and you now live in Greece. Do you feel more Greek or American?" Despina turned toward me. Her eyes begged me to say the right thing, to smooth things over and not make her the girlfriend of an American. But I couldn't lie. "American," I said. "It's where I grew up." Despina looked away. Silence took hold of the table. At least I had told the truth.

*

Three of us at the bank were given an assignment to develop a marketing scheme to attract young adults to Citibank. We had to do most of our work outside of regular working hours. The two women were married with children, so their homes were out of the question. They suggested my place. That's all I needed, for peeping aunt to report a *ménage à trois*. I avoided the question. I asked Despina if we could use her store after hours. She ignored my request. Since Daviko's dinner party, we'd hardly seen each other. With our deadline approaching, I called Victoria to ask for permission. I tried for two days, but nobody was home. I proposed that my co-workers come over the next day—a Friday—after work. At first I was concerned, but these women wore business suits, were at least twice my age, and one was pretty wrinkled. I didn't think peeping aunt would report anything. We took a taxi from the bank to my place and unloaded a big binder, easels and flip charts. I held them up high, hoping peeping aunt would see that these things weren't sex toys.

I set the binder on the kitchen table and looked up stats on our demographic while my co-workers charted the information. The women wanted to develop an ad campaign with photographic images of young adults with hip clothes, scooters, Walkmen, and computers, but I thought showing images of young people at a university would be more appealing.

"That's not how they think here," the wrinkled one said and pointed at the binder. "Look here at what they spend their money on: things, not their future."

"She's right," the other woman said.

An hour into it, the door on the ground floor opened. Feet charged up the marble stairs. I thought it was the dental students.

Victoria and Vasili barged through the door like cops on a drug raid. We were at the kitchen table hovering around the binder. The women jumped.

"See, I told you he was bringing women here," Victoria said, pointing at me.

"What is going on here?" Vasili asked, hands on his hips.

"It's all right," I said to my co-workers and then turned toward Vasili and Victoria. "We're planning a presentation. These are two colleagues from Citibank," I said, laughing inside at their mistake. "I called you many times to ask for permission, but nobody was home."

"We were in Athens," Vasili said.

"Vasili, let's talk in the other room," Victoria said. They went into my bedroom and closed the door. I got a bit nervous, but I hadn't done anything wrong.

My co-workers started to gather their things. "That's not necessary," I said. They ignored my comment and shoved binders into their bags.

Vasili came out. "Can we see you in the back room?"

I nearly said, "You must be kidding," but I bit my tongue and saw the women out before going to the back.

Victoria was leaning against the window looking out.

Vasili folded his arms. "We feel that it would be better if you found another place to live."

"What have I done?" I exploded, throwing my arms in the air. Victoria pointed toward the door. "Those were two married women!"

Vasili waved his hands. "Please, now, let's not—"

"We were working on a bank project, not having a Roman orgy!" Victoria's eyes widened. "It doesn't matter what you were doing; they were here, and others saw. It's not appropriate in my house!"

Vasili waved his hands more. "Please, please—"

"I thought your peeping aunt across the street would be smart enough to see that they were here to work."

"I don't need to take this," she said.

"If you didn't want me to live here, then why'd you agree to it, Victoria?"

"I didn't!"

I stormed out of the room and went to the kitchen. I pushed aside the chairs and paced. Vasili came in.

"Why did you offer me this place if she didn't like the idea?"

"You know how women are."

"Don't give me that, Vasili. When do I have to be out?"

"Victoria would like you out by next weekend."

"You're only giving me a week?"

He nodded. My pulse quickened. I didn't know how to find an apartment in the States, let alone in *Greece*.

*

I called Despina that evening. "I saw it coming," she said. "You should have moved out a long time ago."

"Jesus, Despina, I was just thrown out, and I only have a week to find another place. You could be a bit more understanding."

There was a long pause. "I have to go. Some customers need my help. I'll call you later."

Why was I with a woman who could be so cold?

*

Two days passed and Despina didn't call. I wanted to call her but thought of her lack of sympathy and didn't. A storm had rolled in. I sulked in bed and walked along the foul seaside in the rain. Everything was gray. The road was thick with cars. Nobody else was walking. I didn't care that I got wet. A passenger in a red car blew

cigarette smoke out his window and shouted, "Look at that asshole."
The driver laughed.

I went to Effie and Mary's. When I came in from the rain, my
chest suddenly felt heavy.

"What's wrong?" Effie asked, holding my hands. Worry weighed
down Mary's eyes.

"Tell me what happened, my child," Effie said.

"They kicked me out of the apartment," I managed to say.

Mary covered her mouth.

Effie frowned. "Why?"

I told them about everything but Despina. Talking to them was
like drinking a warm glass of milk.

"That's ridiculous," Effie said. "Shame on Vasili. Shame on him.
You can move in here."

"Yeah, George, you can move in with us!" Mary said, smiling.

"That's a nice offer," I said, wondering how there could be
enough room for me.

"What do you mean, we're family. It's what we do, isn't it?" Effie
said.

Her selflessness really moved me, but I thought about Despina
and the complications that living with Effie and Mary would bring.
It would kill my nightlife. I quickly made up an excuse. "But there's
not enough room for me," I said.

"How isn't there? Mary can sleep with me, and you can sleep in
the bedroom. Or you can sleep in the kitchen, and we can have the
room—Whatever you want." Mary smiled and nodded.

Her proposed sacrifices further struck me, but I couldn't
surrender my private life.

"Knowing that Mary has her studies, I think I should look for
another place, but I'll think about your idea," I said.

"Okay, you think about it. Now let's eat," Effie said, motioning
us to the table.

*

After work the next day, I went into Despina's store. She wasn't
there.

"What time will she be back?" I asked the woman at the register.

"Despina only said that she was leaving." She avoided my eyes.

She always left me word if she was going somewhere. It was crisp and clear out. I walked down Tsimiski thinking about Despina's absence, and her recent lack of understanding, and our differences. She'd been callous, but maybe I had been too selfish, too wrapped up in my own issues. After I found a place, I'd take her to Athens, just the two of us without any distractions.

I had drifted far on Tsimiski, past where I usually turned to go home. At an intersection, I waited for the light to turn green. I daydreamed of Despina and me going to Athens, strolling through the Plaka, eating good food, listening to jazz. In the far lane, Daviko pulled up to the red light with a woman wrapped around him. Neither of them wore a helmet. I couldn't see her face, but she had very short hair. So the guy had met someone, I thought. Now he won't drool all over Despina. He sat upright, looking macho in sunglasses and with the woman holding him tightly. Then she ran her hand through her hair and turned her head. Despina. The light turned green. They took off down an open portion of road, growing smaller and smaller until they were gone.

*

I called in sick. I couldn't risk seeing Despina. I went to different cinemas to watch American movies and returned to the apartment at night when I was sure that sleep would overcome me before loneliness overwhelmed me.

On the third day, I went to Effie and Mary's. I'd come down with a cold. Effie made me *avghou-lemono* soup and put me to bed in Mary's room. I should have been trying to find a place, but I didn't want to. I stayed in bed. Mary and Effie shared the bed in the kitchen and didn't complain.

"When do you have to be out of Vasili's?" Effie asked the next morning.

"Tomorrow," I said, not looking at her. I was pathetic.

When I woke up that afternoon, all my clothes were neatly stacked on the shelves, and my empty suitcases were in the corner.

"What happened?" I asked.

"We moved you out," Effie said.

I sat up in bed. "You did?"

"It was easy," Mary said. "You don't have many things."

"And we cleaned, so you don't have to go back there."

I stared at them feeling uncomfortable. "How can I repay you?"

Effie waved me off.

Part of me didn't want to be so dependent on them. I'd have to change my social habits, but who was I kidding? Despina was gone, and I had no desire to go out. I still wanted to keep my options open for the future, but I couldn't have it all. More than anything, I didn't know how to accept this kind of selflessness. "Thank you," I awkwardly said.

"For what?" Effie said.

*

I went back to work the following week. It was hard to see Despina's store across the street. Late in the day Despina would climb on the back of Daviko's Vespa and scoot in close to him. At first my stomach would turn, but after a while it didn't. Then the bank moved me to a desk away from the window, and I didn't see them at all.

Walking home, I usually passed the old apartment. I didn't miss it. One time I saw Vasili and Victoria's car parked there, so I turned around and went another way.

Most nights Mary would study, and I'd help Effie in the kitchen. I learned how to use a broomstick to roll *filo* dough before layering the delicate sheets to make *spanikopita* and *baklava*. If I didn't do it right, she'd say, "What's that?" with a smile and push me out of the way, like my *mamá* would. We always talked while we worked. Effie would have me tell her about our relatives in the States, and she would tell me about the village during the war, or her husband's family that had never liked her, or about rough winters that had damaged their olive trees. When I told her about stores being open 24-hours a day in *Ameriki*, she said, "How terrible. When do people spend time at home with their families?" When Effie saw that Mary and I were fine on our own, she started to spend more time in Pinakates. Mary and I got along fine, but I missed Effie's company.

Occasionally Mary and I would go out for a coffee. One evening at a sidewalk café on the seaside, I saw Despina and Daviko. They were sitting with their friends at a distant table covered with carafes of retsina and packs of cigarettes. Despina's hair was longer. They all looked very cool—wearing black, legs crossed, probably talking politics. Every few moments I glanced over at their table. They didn't notice me.

Despina and Daviko got up to leave. Arm in arm they walked toward us along a line of tables. Daviko was looking straight ahead and didn't see me, but Despina did. She looked away. When they were close, I said, "Hello."

Despina gave me an upward nod. When Daviko saw me, he stopped. "Georgie, you're still here. I thought you would have returned to your *Ameriki.*" He rubbed Despina's arm. They both looked over at Mary and then back at me.

"No, I'm still here." I turned toward Mary. "This is my cousin. Mary, this is Despina and Daviko."

They didn't move, but Mary did. Wearing the same old sweater, jeans, and shoes, she stood up, smiled, and extended her hand. They shook. "Nice to meet you. How do you all know each other?" Mary asked, looking at me and then back at them.

Despina looked away and Daviko fidgeted.

"I met them when I first came to Thessaloniki," I said. "They helped me see my way."

"How wonderful," Mary said and looked at them.

They stared at her and didn't say anything.

# FLEEING

We were working with a group of ten *mamas*, three of them carrying babies on their backs. The field buzzed with bees, flies, ants, rodents, and snakes, and yet it had a stillness about it. The greenish-gold color of the chest-high savannah grass made the horizon glow. The palms on the hills looked small and insignificant within that sea. Leigh, Jenny, and I overturned weeds with the *mamas*, and the *mamas* sang songs about more rains coming and children eating well and respecting the elders and honoring the dead. The sky was big and the earth rich, and the incoming evening and the singing made the place beautiful, and I was happy to be weeding a field in the middle of Africa.

We didn't finish the field like Leigh wanted, but she told the *mamas* we'd return the next day. "Okay, Mama Leigh. *Merci*," they said and walked away, their colorful wraps beating with every step. We walked toward Leigh's hut feeling dirty and tired and good.

Jenny and I had come to Latumba the day before to work with Leigh for the first time. She'd been in Zaire a year longer than we had. When we rode in on our motos, two barefoot soldiers were outside a row of empty stores with roofs sagging over clucking chickens and resting goats. The soldiers were still there, smoking unfiltered cigarettes and watching us. Soldiers sometimes raped women and got away with it. One looked at Jenny, lowered his M16 to his crotch, and stroked the barrel.

"Pervert," Jenny said under her breath.

"Why are they here, in the bush?" I asked Leigh.

"Those assholes are from here. Sometimes they come back to strut around in their fatigues with their guns," she said, swinging her arm back and forth like a marching soldier. "You'd think they'd take that shit somewhere else. Those stores closed down nine months ago. Two hundred percent hyperinflation's a bitch."

"No kidding," I said. "Two weeks ago in Mopulu, the price of sugar jumped 100 Zaires over a four-hour period."

"Can't let that go, can you, James?" Jenny said, sounding like my boss. She laughed.

*

When Margie had visited my post a few days before, I took her to see a crop I'd planted with *mamas* from my village. The *mamas* wanted to see my boss's reaction to their work. Margie didn't even get out of her red Land Cruiser or take off her Gucci sunglasses. "Looks good. Now it's Happy Hour." She pulled Bloody Mary mix from the back seat. We had two rounds, but I didn't put vodka in mine.

I asked Margie if she wanted to see another crop, but she shook her head. "You're taking this Africa shit too seriously. Lighten up."

I wanted villagers to see me as someone helping them grow food, not someone sipping fancy drinks and eating embassy-bought Wheat Thins. But I played along. Before driving away, Margie leaned out the window and slurred, "I want you and Jenny to work with Leigh for a couple days. Her farming group is one of the tightest in the area. Go have a good time on Uncle Sam." She handed me a bottle of Gilbey's, the same gin my parents drank. I knew Jenny would like it, so I packed it to Latumba yesterday. Our three villages were beads on a string stretched out along the same road, but Leigh's was deep in jungle country.

Tao saw me off when I left. I'd first seen the short kid in the savannah just beyond my property. He was ten years old, had big cheeks and a swayback, and wore a dusty tank top and pair of shorts.

He'd been trapping rats in cone-shaped baskets. I asked him how he knew where to place his traps.

"Near their tracks."

"Where?"

He pointed down at the narrow path. "There, *Monsieur.*"

"I don't see anything."

"*Monsieur*, look."

I dropped to my knees and stared. Eventually I saw tiny indentations in the dirt.

Tao started coming around and asked if I'd help him with his multiplication and French homework. After our lessons, Tao and I sometimes looked at the small world map I'd pulled out of the Air Afrique magazine. He liked that water covered most of the globe, but thought it useless that it was salty. Tao taught me how to trap rats, eat termites and grubs, climb a palm tree. We were pals. Tao was the only villager who never asked me for money or rice or sugar.

"Goodbye, *Monsieur*," he said when I left for Latumba. We high-fived.

"See you in three days."

*

That evening children ran around mud huts playing tag while Jenny loaded Leigh's boom box with Johnny Cash. Her petite body looked good in tight Levis as she danced about. "Sing it, Johnny," she said and sliced the air with her narrow hips.

Leigh stirred the pasta cooking over an open fire and drank Margie's gin. The booze smelled like my parents' liquor cabinet. They'd been good parents, but part of me felt like an outsider. My parents and extended family were fair-skinned English. I was not. They taught me to be distant toward others, but I didn't like it. Something inside of me wanted to be warmer. We didn't hug in my family, but I always liked the idea. I always wondered how I would have been had I not been adopted. Tao made me warmer by leaning up against me when we went over his homework and hugging me sometimes.

Jenny danced over to me and bumped her bony hip against mine. "Come on, tight ass, let's dance."

"I'm helping Leigh with dinner."

"You ain't doing shit," she said, and two-stepped away.

The light was fading. The children had stopped playing, and goats and chickens settled into soft patches of dirt. I'd been in country eight months. At first waking up in a remote African village racked my nerves, but I grew to like the sounds of roosters crowing and *mamas* pounding manioc. I visited Jenny on the weekends. She'd drink or smoke, and maybe I'd smoke too, and we'd listen to rock and country. We knew we were each other's fling. We never talked about being together post-Peace Corps. When I first got to Zaire and saw volunteers' loose ways, I was disgusted. But I didn't know what it was like to live in the bush, in the middle of all that land and with too much time, so much loneliness staring you in the face. I didn't know a few cigarettes, joints, hits of palm wine, or a casual relationship could keep you from cracking up.

I'd get back to Mopulu and spend time with Tao. He would look at pictures of my family and ask about things that seemed so trivial: a chair cushion, some wood siding, a paved street. One hot night, we sat outside. Tao stared at the full moon.

"*Monsieur*, how do they live up there?"

"Who?"

"The people in Apollo."

"You know about *Apollo*?"

"*Eh*, the American before you told me they flew an airplane called Apollo to the moon. How do they live up there?" Tao looked at me with his big brown eyes.

I loved the kid at that moment, as he stared at me, not blinking, softening me as I searched for words to bridge a gap between a society that cooked over fire and one that sent people to the moon.

"*Monsieur*?"

"*Eh*, the Apollo went to the moon, but it came back."

"How did they have enough petrol?"

I smiled. "I don't know, buddy."

\*

Leigh, Jenny, and I ate the pasta next to the dying fire and discussed the ailing country. "President Mobutu's a fucking thief," Leigh said.

To persuade President Mobutu to sell uranium to the States

instead of the Soviets, the U.S. paid Mobutu billions, and he didn't share any of it.

"You'd think there'd be a coup," I said.

"The people are powerless. The soldiers are the only muscle in Zaire," Leigh said. She stood. "I'm going to get my short wave."

I stared at the embers. Most evenings, Tao and I talked at my table. He liked to hear about the differences between our countries. I told him about homelessness in the States. "Why don't those people just knock on someone's door and ask to sleep on their floor, like we do?" he asked.

Leigh returned and clicked on the radio.

*"This is BBC News World Report. In Zaire, rioting has broken out throughout the country."*

We leaned forward.

*"After President Mobutu refused to pay military personnel for the sixth consecutive month, military insurrection has seized the country. Soldiers killed the French Ambassador and other foreign dignitaries and are looting stores and office buildings in Kinshasa, Lubumbashi, Kikwit, and other major cities. The movement appears to be spreading. Foreign refugees are fleeing Zaire. This is all we know at this time."*

We looked at each other.

"Does that mean us?" Jenny asked.

"Yeah," Leigh whispered.

The newsman reported on the war in Bosnia. Cicadas droned in the trees.

"What do we do?" Jenny asked.

"We need to get to Vanga," Leigh said. "We'll leave at sunrise. It's too dangerous to ride through the jungle at night."

I stood up. "I need to brush my teeth."

"You and your teeth," Jenny said. "This country's gone to hell, and you have to brush your teeth."

When I returned, I stared at the embers. With Tao, I'd created a home in Zaire. Before then I wasn't sure if I'd be able to have a family. My time with Tao helped me see that I had it in me.

Leigh stood up. "I need to pack and tell my *domestique* what's going on."

"I'll have to stop at my place before we get to Vanga," Jenny said.

"My village is on the other side of Vanga," I said. "How am I going to get to Mopulu?"

"You'll probably have to forget about all that," Leigh said, walking away.

I felt like I'd been slapped. How could I just leave without saying goodbye to Tao?

Leigh and her *domestique* started crying. Villagers gathered at the edge of Leigh's property and asked, "Why are they crying?" We didn't respond. The two soldiers squeezed through the crowd and headed toward me.

"*Tata*, why are the women crying?"

I held up the bottle. "They drank too much."

Jenny ran toward the latrine, doubled over, and puked. The soldiers laughed. "You *mundeles* are not strong," one said and grabbed the bottle from me. They strutted away.

Jenny returned, and Leigh walked out wiping her eyes. "What happened?"

"I told them that you were both sick from the booze. They believed me because Jenny heaved at the right time."

"I wasn't acting," Jenny said.

"They don't know the news; otherwise they would've mugged us," Leigh said. "But they'll know by tomorrow."

Not being able to see Tao hurt my stomach, but I didn't want to die.

The crowd trailed away and the village became quiet. We sat in silence. I wanted to flee. It was hard to wait. I hoped Tao would understand why I didn't return, but how could he? I thought of my Uncle Richard. At my graduation, he'd said, "Why are you doing something stupid like becoming a *volunteer*? I had my first million before I was thirty." I guess I'd go back to mowing putting greens for Frank, the grounds keeper at Hillcrest Country Club. When I told him I'd joined the Peace Corps, he called me a *fucking liberal*. Some club members considered my joining the Peace Corps *cute*. I'd probably return to that world. It was better than getting shot.

The embers were almost black when we heard the moto. At first it was a far-off buzz that blended with the cicadas, but it gradually got louder. We all stood up. "Jesus, it must be bad if they sent someone at night," Leigh said.

Villagers rushed out of their huts toward the main road and ran alongside the moto as it wound its way to us. It was Tata Mabanza from Vanga. His rubber boots and white helmet were smeared with red mud. "Tata, why did you ride at night?" I asked him. His hand shook as he gave me a note.

"Come to Vanga immediately," I read aloud. "Plane leaves at daybreak. Margie."

Tata Mabanza said the dark jungle and slippery roads made his trip very slow.

"Shit, we have to get out of here," Leigh said and sprinted to her hut.

Villagers surrounded us. Leigh returned and strapped a bag onto her moto. People asked, "Mama Leigh, what is wrong?" Leigh bit her top lip and didn't say anything.

I clicked into task mode. I siphoned gas out of her fuel barrel and was filling our three motos when the soldiers staggered toward us. One carried the empty gin bottle, the other a machete. They asked Tata Mabanza, "Why are you here?" He did not reply. The soldier raised the bottle as if to hit him and laughed when he winced. They walked toward me. I finished filling the tanks and spun on the gas caps.

"Oh God oh God," Jenny whimpered.

The one with the bottle said, "What is wrong here, *mundele?*" His breath reminded me of my parents. The guy with the machete stared down at me.

"The *mademoiselle* is sick. He came to help take her to Vanga."

"They're going to Vanga," people whispered.

The soldiers stared at me. Nobody said anything. The soldiers stood there, the gears in their minds hardly turning.

Leigh walked up, thrust her boom box into one of the soldier's hands, and said, "*Monsieur,* a gift for you."

The soldiers started pushing buttons and didn't look up when we started our bikes. Then Leigh's *domestique* ran out of Leigh's hut with a mound of Leigh's clothes, and everybody understood Leigh was leaving for good.

One soldier yelled, "Stop!" The *domestique* froze. "All of her things are ours now. Drop those clothes." She obeyed.

Some *mamas* from Leigh's farming group said, "Mama Leigh, don't leave."

Leigh hesitated.

"Leigh, we gotta go!" I said, but a soldier grabbed Leigh's handlebars and the one with the machete held my arm. The villagers moved toward the soldiers. The one raised his machete and said, "Get back!" The villagers moved back. I was afraid I'd be hacked up in the middle of Africa. "Give us your money," the soldiers yelled.

We pulled bills from our pockets. One soldier snatched Zaires from Leigh and then grabbed Jenny's left breast before taking her money. None of us moved, but Jenny mumbled, "Fucking asshole."

"What?" he said.

"Nothing."

The villagers were silent as our motorcycles idled. The soldier blew smoke in my face and laughed when I coughed. He took my bills and grabbed my wrist. I tried to pull away, but he squeezed harder. His yellow eyes stared at me as he unfastened my watch.

The other soldier seized Leigh's and Jenny's watches and pulled a knife from his belt. He went to cut Jenny's backpack off her, and she drew back. He placed the knife point under her throat. "You don't move! *D'accord?*"

Tears ran down Jenny's cheeks. He kept the knife at her throat.

"*D'accord?* he said louder.

"*D'accord,*" Jenny said.

The other soldier dumped out Leigh's bag and kicked some Zairian masks across the ground. Leigh clenched her jaw. They ignored Tata Mabanza, and started to count bills. Leigh glanced at us and raised her eyebrows. Jenny and I gave slight nods.

Leigh leaned over, grabbed the wad of bills from a soldier, and tossed it into the air. The bills floated like falling leaves, and the villagers sprang forward. The soldiers yelled, "No! No!" but nobody listened. They lunged at the money, reaching and grabbing.

We took off. Leigh looked back at her *domestique*, who put her hands together like Mother Teresa.

It was pitch black. Leigh led the four of us. Our motos created a deafening roar as we passed through hundreds of villagers lining the road, all of them probably startled and confused because nobody ever drove a motorized vehicle in the Zairian bush at night. Our headlights made the whites of their eyes flash as we passed.

We stopped a kilometer outside of the village, atop an open hill. A full moon had risen. The air was cool and calm. Soft moonlight blanketed the spongy dirt, patches of green grass, and some palms.

Leigh made sure we were okay and then took off, leaving deep tracks behind her. The road dropped into the jungle, dark and dense and humid. I pictured roaches and wide Driver ant trails on the jungle floor, Black Mambas wrapped around branches, and Bonobo monkeys watching us from above. I was glad to be in the middle of the pack. Slick patches of mud sometimes slowed us to a crawl. A couple of times Leigh noticed the mud late, and we all nearly slid out of control. At one point, Jenny's taillight swerved left, then right, and then slammed onto red mud. When I reached her, she was tugging on her bike.

"I'm okay," she said. "Let's keep moving."

We moved. One of us would fall, and we'd re-group. We passed through three villages where more people drawn to the thunder of four motos lined the road. Their country was crumbling, and they had no idea. We rode through walls of jungle, sometimes through valleys, and along green hillsides that shined in silver light that seemed too tranquil to be real. There wasn't the slightest bit of wind.

When wind blew the savannah surrounding Mopulu, the grass rolled like ocean waves. Even then it had that stillness about it. I could watch it for hours. Tao once asked if I'd help hoe a field. A light breeze blew that afternoon, and after the sun dropped, the temperature was cool, and the sky was orange and pink. Five barefoot *mamas* and Tao swung their hand hoes and stepped forward in rhythm. Hoe, step, hoe, step. It was a beautiful motion. I used a large hoe and couldn't keep up, but they didn't say anything. A husband who'd come to keep us company said, "This field is looking very pretty." We were tilling soil, and the husband was telling us a story, when the sound of an airplane surprised us. We shot up.

It was a yellow Cessna. I hadn't seen an airplane in months. It flew low. The white pilot waved and continued toward the fading light, probably heading for Vanga.

We watched the plane until it was gone. The gray light was fading. The husband looked at me. "That's *mundele* work," he said. "You white people work with airplanes. We work with hoes." He pointed at his arm. "This color, it's no good."

Tao looked at me. I wanted to tell him not to believe any of it, that white and black were the same, that people of all colors did incredible things, that he could become a pilot or an astronaut if he wanted. But all I said was, "Airplanes aren't everything."

"They're not, but they're more than a hoe."

I couldn't think of anything to say. I'd never been a quick thinker. I felt like I'd failed Tao. We walked back to the village in the dark.

*

A kilometer from Jenny's village, two burning tires flanked the road, giving the clearing an orange hue. Thick black smoke made it hard to breathe. Three soldiers stepped into the road and stuck out their hands. We stopped. They moved in close. One had a torn white t-shirt tied around his head and gripped two empty liquor bottles by their necks. The other two were shirtless and held M16s. They were barefoot and stunk of vodka.

One holding a machine gun said, "*Mundeles*, give us your money."

"*Monsieur*, we have no money. Other soldiers took it," Leigh said.

He bent down into her face. "You are lying."

Leigh did not flinch or move back. "No, I am not."

He yanked off Leigh's helmet, grabbed her red hair, and yelled, "Give me your money!"

Leigh yelled, "We don't have any money!"

The other soldiers grabbed me and Jenny.

Tata Mabanza revved his moto and started honking and circling us. The soldiers yelled, "Stop! Stop!" They let go of us. Tata Mabanza took off down the road, and they ran after him yelling.

Leigh screamed, "Let's go!" and sped away, swerving around the soldiers before they regrouped. I took off and Jenny followed. The soldiers stood in a line up ahead, waving their arms and guns. They'd kill us if we stopped. I accelerated through the first three gears. The soldiers shouted, "Stop! Stop!" but I cranked the throttle all the way back. They shot bullets into the sky, and then pointed their guns at me. I ducked, expecting them to shoot, but they jumped aside as I kept my head down and rode through them, shifting into fourth gear. In my mirror I saw them regroup. They waved their arms and pointed their guns at Jenny, but she didn't stop either, and again they jumped out of the way as she passed. I felt relieved until I saw flashes and a string of shots peppering the ground to my left. I screamed and ducked lower, expecting to get hit in the back, but that didn't happen. I looked in my mirror; Jenny was still behind me. We kept riding.

Two clicks later we pulled into Jenny's yard. I killed my bike and Leigh hollered, "James!" I ran to Jenny. She shook violently and cried.

I tried to help Jenny off her moto, but she wouldn't let go of the handlebars. We pried her hands free and lifted her off. She stayed in the sitting position and sobbed as we carried her inside the hut.

I lit two candles. We elevated Jenny's legs and covered her. Tata Mabanza sat against the wall, his head in his hands. Jenny wept. I held her shoulder and Leigh said, "You're safe now." I couldn't produce saliva.

Leigh had a black eye. My hands shook and my head hurt. I tried to drink some water, but my throat was baked shut. I sipped a few drops and watched a candle burn. I thought about the shots. My father had told me about the ground at Normandy dancing from machine-gun fire.

"We should leave soon," Leigh said. "The note said '*immediately.*'"

"*Mademoiselle*, at night we cannot see the hippopotamuses in the river," Tata Mabanza said. "We will leave at first light."

"*D'accord*," Leigh said

Jenny fell asleep. My head throbbed, and my throat stayed dry. I saw the flashes of machine-gun fire and thought of my parents. My hands shook. At this point getting to Mopulu didn't matter. I wanted to go home.

Tata Mabanza stretched out along the wall. "I don't understand you Peace Corps Volunteers. When my country needs you most, you leave."

Leigh and I looked at each other and then looked down. He

was right.

When the sky turned gray, we headed to the Kwilu River. Mist enshrouded the chestnut-colored river. Fires burned on the other side at Vanga. Pirogues shuttled us across. Margie stood on the bank. She looked like hell.

"Soldiers ransacked the clinic last night and drank rubbing alcohol till they were sick. The villagers ran them out."

"Why all the fires?" asked Leigh.

"So that the plane can spot Vanga in this mist."

"It's not here yet?" I asked.

"Not yet."

"Do I have time to go to Mopulu?"

She shook her head. "Absolutely not. Nobody is to leave Vanga. State Department order."

"But it's only 45 clicks away. I can be back in two hours. I have to—"

"No," Margie snapped. "If you leave I'll report you as AWOL."

I buried my face in my hands. Tata Mabanza was right about us. The least I could do was say goodbye to Tao and give him my things.

Leigh touched my shoulder. "Don't worry, your villagers will work it out."

"I have food in the Land Cruiser," Margie said. "It's near the landing strip. I'll meet you there after I use the latrine."

Leigh and Jenny started toward the landing strip, but I didn't move. "Coming?" Leigh asked.

"Yeah, I'll be there."

When Margie closed the latrine door, I kick-started my moto and took off for Mopulu. I didn't think Margie would leave without me, but I still rode full throttle and watched for the plane the whole way. When I pulled into Mopulu, Tao ran to my yard smiling. "You're back early!"

I didn't remove my helmet. I pushed my bike to my barrel of fuel. I sucked on the rubber hose and shoved it into the gas tank.

"*Monsieur*, why are you doing that? You just got home."

Tao's eyes held kilos of worry. I looked down and stared blankly until petrol spilled over my gas tank and onto the ground.

"*Monsieur?*"

I screwed the barrel shut. I walked around the hut and into my home. Tao followed. I sat on my bed and removed my helmet.

"*Monsieur?*"

I looked down at my mud-smeared boots. "Tao, I have to leave."

"Where are you going, *Monsieur?*"

I took a deep breath. "I have to return to America."

"But why, *Monsieur?*"

"My boss told me I have to go."

"When will you come back home?"

I shook my head.

He sat down next to me and put a hand on my shoulder. "You're not coming back?"

I shook my head.

"Why, *Monsieur?*"

I couldn't answer him.

I stood up but he didn't. I stuffed my journal and passport into an empty flour sack, and went to Tao. I grabbed his arm and whispered, "Listen buddy, after I leave, don't tell *anyone* I'm not coming back." He didn't blink. "If they know, they will take all my things. I want you to have everything. You must move it all tonight, when everybody is sleeping. The others will know tomorrow."

I let go of him and pulled a box of money from my dresser. I placed it in his hand. "Go to the market tomorrow and buy rice, salted fish, beans, chickens, a goat, and batik for your mother. Do not buy things that will spoil. And do not save this money—it won't be good next week. Understand?"

He nodded.

"And you must continue to study, so you can leave someday."

"How *Monsieur?* How without you?" He stood with his arms to his sides, shaking his head. "If I leave here, how will I find you?" Tears ran down his face.

My eyes got watery. We looked into each other's eyes, neither of us saying anything.

Eventually I said, "Tao, will you do all this for me, buddy?"

Tao wiped his eyes and nodded. We sat down on the bed. I put my arm around him. He leaned into me. Our chests rose and fell together. I wanted to sit there next to Tao long into the night, holding that moment, but I pictured the plane landing at Vanga and Margie being mad enough to leave without me. I looked at the door, then at Tao. I pressed the key into his hand. "Remember to lock the door."

He held my hand and we walked outside.

I strapped the flour sack onto my moto. Tao closed the door and secured the padlock. He stood, hands at his sides, looking very alone. I wanted to take him with me, but our worlds spun in different solar systems. I hated that mine included an exit ticket and his didn't.

I kick-started my bike. I pulled away and sped out of Mopulu. The sun was rising at my back. I followed my shadow down a long stretch of sandy road that cut through still savannah.

# About the Author

**Dimitri Keriotis** was raised in Northern California. He served as a Peace Corps Volunteer in Zaire and Bolivia. His stories have appeared or are forthcoming in *Beloit Fiction Journal*, *Georgetown Review*, *Evening Street Review*, *Flyway*, *BorderSenses*, and elsewhere. He teaches English at Modesto Junior College and co-coordinates the High Sierra Institute. He and his family live in the foothills of the Sierra Nevada. Visit him online at www.dimitrikeriotis.com.

CPSIA information can be obtained at www.ICGtesting.com
Printed in the USA
BVOW07s1841161014

371030BV00001B/5/P